"I'll not let you waste your life."

Michael swung her around to face him, continuing savagely, "Kit's always taken what he wants and to hell with the consequences, but I thought you had more sense. It seems I was wrong."

"It seems we were both wrong!" declared Nicola. A voice in her head was screaming, *How could he think such a thing if he really loved me?*

She asked stonily, "Is that all, Michael?"

"No!" His eyes blazed into hers as he pulled her roughly to him and crushed his lips down on hers. When he broke the kiss, he went on harshly, "I've always known I should keep well away from you. I should have trusted my instincts." He let her go. "I covet Kit's good fortune, but refuse to share your favors."

"No one's asking you to!"

Books by Jacqueline Gilbert

HARLEQUIN PRESENTS

160—DEAR VILLAIN
600—A HOUSE CALLED BELLEVIGNE
801—CAPRICORN MAN

HARLEQUIN ROMANCE

2102—EVERY WISE MAN
2214—COUNTRY COUSIN
2308—SCORPIO SUMMER
2492—THE TRODDEN PATHS
2631—THE CHEQUERED SILENCE

These books may be available at your local bookseller.

Don't miss any of our special offers. Write to us at the following address for information on our newest releases.

Harlequin Reader Service
P.O. Box 52040, Phoenix, AZ 85072-2040
Canadian address: P.O. Box 2800, Postal Station A,
5170 Yonge St., Willowdale, Ont. M2N 6J3

JACQUELINE GILBERT

capricorn man

Harlequin Books

TORONTO • NEW YORK • LONDON
AMSTERDAM • PARIS • SYDNEY • HAMBURG
STOCKHOLM • ATHENS • TOKYO • MILAN

In memory of
my parents
Madge and Ben Gilbert

Harlequin Presents first edition July 1985
ISBN 0-373-10801-X

Original hardcover edition published in 1985
by Mills & Boon Limited

Printed in U.S.A.

CHAPTER ONE

THE Brahms Symphony drew to a close and over the fading applause the announcer's voice informed listeners that they had been hearing a repeat of a broadcast given the previous year from the Royal Albert Hall by the visiting New York Symphony Orchestra, conductor Cornelius Webber.

Neil! Nicola Redford gave a gasp of delighted surprise and put down the page of manuscript she was correcting. What a coincidence! She found she was smiling and remembered Neil as she had seen him only two days previous, an arm around her mother's shoulders as they waved her goodbye from Kennedy Airport.

Nicola stretched and leaned back against the pillows, thinking what a lot had happened in the past year ... since Neil had erupted into their lives. Nearing sixty, his thick hair silver-grey, his face a little craggy, but his reputation as a conductor and musician precluding any claims to the passing years. As Neil had wryly told her, conductors never retire, they are carried off the rostrum protesting!

From her step-father, Nicola's thoughts turned to her mother, Adele. Abandoned by her husband when Nicola was a baby and widowed some years later, Adele Redford had struggled to make a living as a musician, going where the work was, she and her child living out of a suitcase in digs and cheap hotel rooms. Eventually Adele realised that a more stable up-bringing was required and, with financial help from her sister's husband, Nicola was sent to a boarding school and spent weekends and holidays at Bredon House, the home of her Auntie Joan. Those early years had enforced a strong independent spirit in Nicola and as Adele gained stature in the music world Nicola's life was divided into three very separate channels. School was suffered because it had to be and her mad-cap exploits landed her into constant trouble, but she was bright, giving her attention to those subjects she liked. Bredon House was a tantalising glimpse of what family life was about and showed how much she wanted to belong. But her visits to Adele were the highlights, and as girlhood was left behind the fierce loyalty to her mother was strengthened by an awareness of Adele's good sense and calm disposition and she longed to be more like her. This was a high goal. Nicola was impulsive and far from calm, and had a propensity for landing herself into trouble. She had a restless spirit and an enquiring mind and hated to be tied down to one job. When Cornelius Webber came into her mother's life, Nicola was delighted.

Neil was invited to be guest conductor with the orchestra in which Adele was leader. He was in England to give a series of concerts all over the country. According to Adele he was a bear during rehearsals, exacting yet brilliant and inspiring. Afterwards, when he amazingly asked her out to dinner, she found he wasn't such a bear after all, and before she knew it, Adele was swept off her feet, married and taken to America. It was second-time marriage for them both. Neil's first wife and child had been killed in a car accident after only three years and he had thrown himself into his work, never considering re-marrying, until the attractive first violinist caught his eye. As for Adele, she had long ago thought such a thing as middle-age romance was not for her.

Nicola watched the whirlwind courtship from the sidelines and had eventually bullied her mother into marriage, once she realised Adele's heart was involved. A year later Nicola was persuaded to visit them in New England and stayed for three months. Neil tried to encourage the idea of Nicola staying indefinitely, delighted with his ready-made daughter and was most persuasive.

'It would make your mother very happy if you decided to make your home here,' he said, choosing his words with care. 'We could get you a nice apartment in Manhattan where you could carry on with your writing—inspiration isn't confined to England, is it? Will you think about it, Nickie, mmm? You've enjoyed your time here with us, haven't you?'

Nicola said quickly, 'Neil, you know I have.'

'Then why don't you stay?' He pursed his lips consideringly. 'Is there someone special back home? Adele thinks not, but it wouldn't be the first time a parent was kept in the dark.' His grey eyes regarded her quizzically and she shook her head.

'No. No-one special. I sometimes wonder if I ever will get married.'

Neil gave a snort of disbelief. 'That's a pretty drastic thing to say, especially at your age. My goodness, life's just beginning to get interesting, and you've certainly packed a lot of living into your twenty-eight years so far—and I can't believe you've never been asked!' He looked at her belligerently, as if defying her to argue and Nicola began to chuckle.

'Thank you for the compliment, Neil. As a matter of fact, I have been asked, a few times, actually. I'm probably choosy.'

'Honey, when you do meet up with the right man you'll know for sure. Well—we'll let you go, but only if you promise to visit us regularly and if you're ever in trouble, we're here.'

The talk with Adele was conducted with her mother's usual good sense and calm.

'I'm sad you're going, but I do understand,' Adele admitted. They were walking along the shore of Long Island Sound, spending Nicola's last day on the water. Neil waved from the small sailing boat and they both waved back. 'I'm slightly concerned, Nicola, that the flat won't be vacant for you.'

'Oh, that's no problem,' Nicola assured her cheerfully. 'I shall give the tenants a chance to look round for something else and stay with Jennie and Bill Lambert for the time being.'

'Shall you go to Bredon House to see them all? If you do, give them my love.' Adele frowned. 'We have so little family back in England, but if you do need help or advice Michael will help.'

'Does he still write to you, Mother?'

'Now and again—just to keep in touch.'

'I'd sooner ask Kit. Michael and I have a wary truce these days, but even so, I'd sooner go to Kit.'

'My sympathy lies entirely with Michael,' informed Adele dryly. 'You used to lead him a wretched dance as a child. Have you told either of the boys about your book yet?'

Nicola smiled at the thought of the Dalmain cousins being termed 'boys' and shook her head. 'I rarely see Michael, you know, and as for Kit, I'll wait until Dalmains accept my next book before unveiling myself.' She turned her face into the breeze, narrowing her eyes from the glare of the sun on the water, her hair streaming out behind her. 'I can't wait to see Kit's face when he finds out who his new author is!' She laughed and turned back to her mother. 'I can hardly believe it myself.'

'My dear, I can,' Adele told her. 'You've always been inventive, always had a liking for scribbling stories even as a child. I'm not at all surprised you've written a book and I'm very proud of you, and so is Neil.'

Nicola put an arm round her diminutive mother. 'I'll send you both a copy, duly signed,' she promised, grinning at the idea.

'I shall look forward to that, darling.' Adele paused in her stride. 'Have we gone far enough, do you think?' They turned and her eyes sought her husband coming towards shore in his boat and rested on the young man helping him. 'Do we have to ask that young man to dinner, do you think, Nickie?'

Nicola chuckled, watching with appreciative eyes as the dinghy swept smoothly into harbour. 'I shouldn't think so. This one isn't a potential husband like all the rest Neil's paraded before me while I've been here, he's only been taken on to crew for him. Poor Neil! All his match-making plans gone for nought. No, we'll have our last evening together, just the three of us, mmm?'

The telephone rang out shrilly, bringing Nicola sharply back from Westport, Connecticut, to Bredon House, Ashwell, Surrey. Switching off the radio she stretched out a hand, picked up the receiver and was about to speak when a voice the other end said, 'Miss Golding, I'm back. Any chance of a pot of tea?' and before she could speak the line went dead.

Michael Dalmain. Not changed much, Nicola thought wryly. Still giving orders under the disguise of requests and expecting them to be carried out! Her lips suddenly curved into a gleeful smile. Here she was, barely arrived back in England and contrary to her mother's prediction, she was helping Michael, rather than the other way about!

Not that he knows it yet, Nicola pondered, throwing off the covers and swinging her legs out of the bed. And I bet he doesn't much like the idea, her thoughts went on, as she reached for the kimono she used as a house-coat. Tying the belt, she eyed herself in the mirror deciding she was decent enough for the conventions—the kimono was all-enveloping and the silk pyjamas could have been worn to a party without anyone raising an eyebrow. She leaned forward and peered at her face critically. No make-up, but then, she wasn't trying to impress Michael. When someone had seen you looking your worst many times in the past there wasn't much point in trying to eradicate that memory. She gave a laughing sigh and wondered, ruefully, why her mother's beauty had passed her by. Instead of glorious dark auburn hair she was landed with a colour neither one thing nor the other. Butterscotch, one imaginative swain had once called it and when the sun streaked it fair it could look quite interesting. It was thick, that was something, and Nicola quickly ran a comb through it, carelessly tucking the shoulder-length style behind her ears, out of the way. And where were Adele's fantastic green eyes she mourned, glaring at her own nondescript hazel belligerently. But the thing that really grieved her was that she had absolutely none of Adele's musical talent! From her shadowy father she had inherited her height and temper, the former philosophically accepted by her late teens, the latter severely sat upon and more or less controlled throughout her adult life. From whom, she wondered, making her way down the stairs, had she got the hankering to write?

The kitchen was pleasantly warm, the Aga banked low for the night. As she made the tea she remembered trying to sort out the Dalmain family for Neil when he had questioned her about her relatives back in England.

'It's a bit complicated,' she admitted. 'Mother's younger sister, Joan, married a widower, John Dalmain, whose first wife died after bearing him a son. Michael, the son, was thirteen when this second marriage took place and eventually Noel and Cassandra were born—they are my true cousins. Uncle John was a partner in Dalmains Publishing and he and Auntie Joan set off in a small aircraft piloted by a friend to go to Edinburgh to attend a book fair. The plane crashed in fog and there were no survivors.'

Neil gave a grunt of sympathy and Nicola went on: 'Michael was twenty-six when this happened, training to be a barrister. Noel was . . . oh, let me think . . . ten, and Cassie must have been six. Michael became their guardian and Bredon House became his base but he keeps a flat in London and divides his time between there and Ashwell which is an hour's train journey from the city.' She gave a pensive sigh. 'I was just turned twenty-one when they died and I couldn't believe it. They were closer to me than a normal aunt and uncle.'

'How old are the children now?' Neil asked and Nicola thought for a moment. 'Noel must be coming up for his eighteenth birthday and Cassandra is fourteen. I must say, Michael has been extremely good with them—organising his life around them can't be easy.'

'Is he married?'

Nicola shook her head. 'No. Neither of them are. The Dalmains don't seem to marry young.'

Neil frowned. 'You've lost me, Nicola.'

She chuckled. 'Sorry. I meant Michael and his cousin Kit. Uncle John was in partnership with his brother, Rupert, and Kit's his son. He's joined Uncle Rupert into the business and they've just accepted my book.'

'So you're not totally without family in England,' observed Neil.

'Well, only Noel and Cassandra are real family but the Dalmains have allowed me to adopt them all. I used to have wonderful holidays at Bredon House. It's a lovely place, old with plenty of character and as it's right on the edge of Ashwell you feel as though you're in the country—a marvellous spot for children to grow up in. We had such adventures—Michael, Kit and I. They didn't really want me, but they had no choice as I just tagged on behind!'

The first time they met she had been tall for her eight years, thin and bony, with tawny cropped hair on which was pulled a jaunty sailor's cap. She was wearing a tartan shirt, jeans and a denim jacket, canvas shoes on her feet. From the back she looked like a boy, and such was the obvious intention, but when she turned full face, her true sex was evident. The bone structure was too finely drawn, the features too delicate for her to be anything but female. She was not pretty, but the discerning could see something in her that augered well for the future—the hazel eyes flecked with gold, the curve of the cheek, the wide, sensitive mouth.

'Who is she?' asked the fair boy curiously, and the dark boy scowled and said dismissively:

'Joan's niece.'

The girl gave the fair boy a friendly gamine grin and said: 'I'm Nickie. What's your name?'

The fair boy grinned back. 'Kit. I'm Michael's cousin.'

'I'm Michael's cousin, too,' the girl Nicola replied proudly. The dark boy's scowl deepened and he said bluntly, 'No, you're not. We're no relation.' He turned and began to walk away. The boy Kit laughed, but not unkindly, and ran to catch up with his cousin. After a few seconds Nicola set her jaw and pushing clenched fists into her pockets, began to follow them, steadily, and with determination. She grinned as she remembered. 'Kit was easy-going—he still is—and didn't much care, but I used to make Michael furious and we became deadly enemies. I hated being a girl and only liked doing adventurous things, which usually were dangerous and Michael had the devil's own job of bringing me back alive!'

Nicola was still smiling at the memory as she carried the tea tray along the corridor to the room Michael used as an office. She tapped at the door and edged herself and the tray through, shutting the door behind her with the heel of her foot.

She waited a moment, letting her eyes become accustomed to the semi-darkness. Michael was sitting at his desk reading a letter, a solitary lamp throwing sufficient light for the job. He murmured, without looking up: 'Thank you, Miss Golding,' as she made her way to the side table. By his appearance he had been to some important function, for he was dressed in evening suit, though the tie was now loosened, the top button of the white shirt undone and the jacket hung round the back of the chair.

Nicola regarded this man she had known for so long with renewed curiosity. He must be thirty-three, she reckoned, doing a quick mental arithmetic, and pouring out the tea she conceded that Michael was someone you noticed, even if his type of looks were not the kind that turned you on. He had the Dalmain broad forehead and long, straight nose, the wide cheekbones that brought a hollow to the cheeks and a strong, rather square jawline, dented at the chin with a distinctive cleft. Cool, blue eyes, she knew, were set below a straight brow and a well-shaped skull was covered with thick, dark hair. An extremely mobile mouth with a thinnish upper lip completed what was a striking, rather than a handsome, face. As a barrister, this eye-catching face allied to a tall, lean frame, and a voice that could, when needed, be used like an actor's, gained considerable advantage in court. What was even more important, he had a keen, agile brain. When Michael Dalmain was at his most charming and persuasive in court it was usually when he was to be most feared. Generally speaking he was a very private person with tremendous self-control. Nicola found that once they had left childhood behind they managed to conduct themselves with passable equanimity. Even now she had the urge to test his self-control to the limit, but it was only because what she termed his enigmatic, inscrutable look drove her wild. She knew that beneath the relaxed, polite mask there was a force to be reckoned with, having in the past borne the brunt of both verbal and physical attacks. Certainly implacable politeness and an amused tolerance, his usual attitude towards herself, were difficult weapons to overcome.

Perhaps now was the time to find out what really made Michael tick, to lay aside the cudgels. If he accepted her help they would be working and living together closely. *If* he accepted her help— there was a strong possibility that he would refuse it!

As she took the cup to the desk she realised that like most faces one has known well since childhood she took Michael's for granted. Tonight her perception seemed sharper, more aware. Maturity had given depth to his features and she grudgingly admitted that the tales Kit related of Michael as a lady-killer could easily be believed ... although Kit was a fine one to talk, but his amours were open and flagrantly whirlwind.

She put the cup down on the desk noticing, as the light from the lamp caught it, the small scar above his right eye where, swinging a cricket bat with misguided energy, Nicola had once knocked him unconscious.

Hearing the chink of china Michael glanced up, saying again, 'Thank you ...' and even as his eyes were back to the letter, and he continued, '... anything to report?' his brain registered and his head shot up. Eyes darkening with surprise and a patch of colour marking his cheek bones, Michael allowed the stunned expression of disbelief only a momentary possession and assumed his usual one of cool scrutiny, saying: 'Hello, Red ... to what

do I owe this honour?' His mouth pulled down at
the edges as he added, 'I fear the worst.'

She had never managed to train him into
abandoning the nickname 'Red'. It had started,
early on, as a shortening of Redford, the use of
surnames being peculiar to boys. It had been
strengthened when she had experimented with a
hair dye in an attempt to reproduce her mother's
auburn colouring. It went disastrously wrong and
she had to live with bright magenta tresses which
took weeks to wash out. It was not in her nature
to hide and she brazened it out, fighting anyone
who made fun of her, sometimes having to be
rescued by Michael, who in turn ended up fighting
her opponent. As she developed from a scrawny
kid into a slim, attractive teenager, the boys were
less inclined to tease, wanting her favours more
than her fists . . . all but Michael, who still insisted
on calling her Red. Kit had been the only one to
give her comfort through the magenta hair ordeal
and even reckoned it suited her. This she might
have been able to accept had her neck and face
escaped contamination as well as her hair. Auntie
Joan, hiding her amusement, produced the
necessary creams and ointments and her skin,
thankfully, returned to normal well before her
hair.

'How unfair of you,' Nicola now replied calmly.
'Hello, Michael. I can't remember if you take
sugar.' And she put the sugar bowl by the side of
the cup.

Michael pushed back his chair and rose to his
feet, moving round the desk, switching on another
lamp as he came forward. For a split second
Nicola thought he was going to give her a
welcoming kiss, but he merely placed his hands

upon her shoulders and drew her more clearly into the circle of light. 'You're looking very well, Red.' His hands left her shoulders. 'I thought you were in the States?'

If it had been Kit or Noel, Nicola thought, I would have got the kiss and a hug too. One of these days, Michael Dalmain, she promised herself, I'm going to pierce that damned reserve you've built up, just for the hell of it!

'I've been back a couple of days. I'm an angel of mercy,' she replied, and on an impulse lifted her face to his and gave him a token kiss on the cheek. She felt him freeze and withdraw slightly and gave a mental shrug. What had she expected? Rome wasn't built in a day.

'I've thought you many things in my time, Red, but can't ever recall seeing you in a celestial light before.' Michael's voice was dry as he hitched himself against the edge of the desk, looking at her warily.

She said kindly, 'There's always a first time,' and walked back to the tray, collecting her own cup and sitting down in a nearby wing-chair. Voice pensive, she asked, 'You didn't think I was an angel of mercy when I ran three miles home for help when you broke a leg in Worrel Caves?'

'Certainly not,' came the prompt reply. 'It was your fault for getting lost in the damned caves in the first place . . . if you cast your mind back.'

'I might have caused you to be in that particular place, at that particular time,' reasoned Nicola, 'but I can't actually remember pushing you down the cliff face.'

'Why I didn't murder you as a child I'll never know,' Michael remarked pleasantly. 'What are you doing here, Red?' He paused. 'Where is Miss Golding?'

'Aren't you pleased to see me?' she asked, with deep reproach in her voice. Michael eyed her thoughtfully, a number of replies obviously whirling around in his head. He contented himself with:

'The pleasure of your company is marred slightly by memories of the havoc that usually follows.'

She grinned. 'Ah, come on, Michael, that's years ago. Can't you see me as a sophisticated, responsible twenty-eight-year-old? Other people can.'

A brow quirked, but Michael seemed unimpressed as his eyes travelled over her, one pyjama clad leg crossed over the other, slippered foot dangling. 'Why aren't you in America?' he asked with patient persistence.

'Do you want me to go into personal reasons, or are you really asking why I'm here?' She judged she had gone far enough. A warning light was flickering in those cool, blue eyes. She went on: 'Cassandra 'phoned me.'

Michael stared, eyes narrowing, and then swung himself from the desk and round into the chair. 'And what has Cassandra done now?' he asked in a resigned voice.

'Not much, from what I can gather,' observed Nicola. 'You are, however, without a secretary-cum-housekeeper-cum companion, or whatever it is Miss Golding liked to call herself.'

Silence greeted this. Michael's lids dropped lower, hiding his expression and after a moment ran fingers through his hair before lifting his head to say, with great restraint: 'Miss Golding is my secretary, paid to live in so that there is another female in the house for Cassandra's sake.'

'I see. Well . . . Miss Golding is no more. I think it more than likely that Cass's acquisition of a baby bat helped her along her way.'

Another silence while Michael digested this snippet of information. He said presently, 'Explain, please.'

'Certainly, if you will drink your tea. I'm sure you don't like it cold and I'm damned if I'm going to get up in the middle of the night, slave over a hot kettle, and see my results go to waste.'

With great forebearance Michael took up the cup, grimacing at the first sip, adding a spoon of sugar before downing the lot. He said irritably: 'It's hardly the middle of the night. If I saw her light was on, and I asked, Miss Golding never minded brewing up for me.'

'I bet she didn't,' murmured Nicola dryly and received a sharp look. She went on, 'I have a letter from the estimable Miss Golding which will, no doubt, explain that her mother is ill. She might even mention the bat.' She pulled out the letter from the kimono pocket and waved it in the air.

Michael rose and fetched it, ripping open the envelope while Nicola watched with unconcealed interest. He scanned the contents and threw the letter down on the desk, taking up his cup and pouring out more tea.

Nicola waited a second or two and then complained, 'I hope you're not going to keep what she says to yourself! Does she mention the bat?'

'Among other things—a white mouse, a jackdaw and a grass-snake, the latter heavily underlined.'

Nicola began to giggle and then bit her lip. From his expression Michael was not amused. The loss of Miss Golding was obviously a crisis. 'You know what Cass is like regarding creatures great and small—and you won't let her have a dog,' she said.

Michael gave an exasperated exclamation. 'It's not that I won't, it's just not practical. You can't expect a secretary to be responsible for a dog when we're all out most of the day and Victor has enough to do, running the house, and anyway . . .' He stopped.

Nicola finished, '. . . Miss Golding can't stand animals.'

Michael clattered the china down on the tray. 'Damn the woman! She was a good secretary, but . . .'

'. . . couldn't stand teenagers.'

Michael's lips tightened and then a reluctant smile softened them. 'Everything seemed fine at the beginning,' he said a little wearily and Nicola observed:

'Until she began to realise that the possibility of becoming the mistress of the house was rather remote.'

Michael's head swung round. 'Did Cassandra tell you this, Red?'

Nicola decided to ignore the prosecuting voice. 'No, Michael. Noel did.'

'The woman was forty-five if she was a day.' His voice was dismissive.

'My dear Michael, what difference does that make? The whole situation shouted out for the poor thing to fall for you. There's such a romantic idea about a lonely barrister, fighting for justice, coming home exhausted from winning his case and finding comfort available with a pot of tea and a sympathetic hand soothing his fevered brow.'

Michael's mouth twitched, the rigidity in his face muscles relaxing. 'I'm hardly lonely. You're forgetting Cassandra and Noel. And Victor is a force to be reckoned with.'

And more than a pot of tea somewhere in London, thought Nicola. Poor Miss Golding. 'Is she coming back? Miss Golding?' she asked. Michael slowly shook his head and Nicola mentally crossed her fingers. 'Good,' she said. 'How about me?'

Michael froze, weighing her up. His hands, nice hands, Nicola noticed and remembered—long, broad fingers with healthy square nails, these fingers now interlaced, resting on the desk. 'What,' he asked, 'exactly do you mean?' The phrasing was carefully precise.

'I mean exactly what I say. Would *I* do?' Michael made no effort to reply and she went on matter-of-factly: 'I am, at the moment, without accommodation. I can type, do shorthand and while I know you have little respect for my capabilities in general, I can run a household, especially one that has Victor in it. I am extremely polite on the 'phone and reliable at taking down messages. I wipe my feet on the mat and hang up wet towels. I'm not a secret gin drinker . . . I even enjoy the company of teenagers and white mice.' She smiled encouragingly.

Voice impassive, Michael said: 'You can't possibly want to work for me, Red . . . and you know your room is available whenever you want it.'

A wave of dull red swept her face. How sneaky of him to be so damned politely kind.

'I'm not destitute, Michael—and why can't I want to work for you?'

'Why didn't you stay on in America? I know Adele had hopes in that direction.'

Nicola sighed. Her colour had now returned to normal. 'I feel that the judge should break in here and say "would our learned friend kindly stick to the question asked!" I didn't stay in America because I didn't want to, and a job is a job. It will give you a breathing space and the kids a break from strangers. You wouldn't object if I went to Town occasionally, would you? I need to call in at the office and sign cheques . . . and I might have some other typing to do, but I'd make sure yours was done first.' She felt her colour rising again and went on lightly: 'For heaven's sake, Michael, if the idea repels you, say so! I'm sure I can find you someone as competent as Miss Golding who likes animals and teenagers as well.'

'Don't jump to conclusions, Red,' drawled Michael. 'If you're serious, your idea seems an admirable one.'

'It does?' echoed Nicola, taken aback.

'Yes, but we must keep things on a professional footing.'

Recovered, Nicola said briskly: 'Naturally. Much easier for you to boot me out when you've had enough of me.'

'That wasn't what I meant,' he replied brusquely. 'If you won't accept free bed and board then I certainly won't accept a free secretary.' His jaw clamped. 'You really are the limit, Red.'

'I always have been where you're concerned,' returned Nicola cheerfully, 'and don't be so touchy, Michael. You misjudge me. I'm merely putting it on record that when you can't stand the sight of me around any longer, when the limit is stretched to breaking point, you have my permission to say clear out. It works both ways. I shall soon tell you when I've had enough. At the moment it suits us both.' She paused and added mischievously: 'I promise to be on my best behaviour.'

'Heaven forbid.' The corners of his mouth turned up and his eyes smiled. 'As for suiting us both, with Noel and Cassandra part of the deal I think I'm getting the better bargain.'

She laughed, the smile lingering on her face. 'How are they? I've only seen them briefly today.'

'Living up to the teenage image. Existing in a world of their own and only surfacing when they want something. Noel's being particularly awkward. I don't seem to be able to do or say anything right where he's concerned. Cassandra is liveable with, apart from the wretched waifs and strays she picks up. This bat thing will have to be looked into.'

'I gather she found it injured. I don't think she expects to keep it,' offered Nicola placatingly, 'and if she's intending to train to become a vet what's more natural than keeping a menagerie?'

'I rather think Cass has had no small part in getting rid of Miss Golding. She'll be delighted when she realises she has you to take her place.'

Nicola thought it expedient to change the subject. She said: 'And you, Michael, your reputation is growing. I hear about your successes from Kit and the children. If ever I find myself in the dock I shall ask you to defend me.'

'I doubt you'll need me, Red. You'll talk your way easily round the judge.'

She dimpled. 'Cassandra told me you were at Court today. Did you win your case?'

'I did—not that I think he deserved to get off.'

'Michael!' exclaimed Nicola, in mock horror, 'do you mean to tell me that you defend even when you suspect your client to be guilty?'

'A job is a job,' mimicked Michael, 'and don't forget the jury, will you? By the way, how are Adele and Neil?'

'Very well and very happy. It's lovely to see them together, not that either of them are demonstrative, it's just their look of surprise that this should have happened to them at their time of life.'

'I'm glad. Is Adele working?'

'She's done a few recitals but I think she's enjoying just being a wife. The house in Fairfield County, Connecticut, is lovely, old and colonial, but it needs a woman's touch and mother's in her element. Neil gives her a free rein. It's good to know she's being looked after for a change. Her life hasn't been easy, but she's never complained, and Neil's determined to make it up to her.'

'She's a resourceful woman, your mother, and talented. I admire her.'

'Do you, Michael?' Nicola gave a wry smile. 'The feeling is mutual. She's told me often enough.'

'Poor Red,' he drawled, 'how annoying having me thrust down your throat.'

'Yes, it is, rather.' Nicola went pensive. 'It's difficult to imagine her falling for someone like my father. A light-hearted, irresponsible charmer, so I'm told, and volatile . . . and she's so tranquil and level-headed.'

'Love is a fever that can strike the most unlikely people,' Michael observed cynically and Nicola raised her brows, saying:

'You want to be careful, Michael—they reckon it hits the cynics harder.' She rose and collected the sugar basin from the desk eyeing his evening suit. 'You look as though you've been wining and dining.'

'A dreary dinner honouring a retiring judge.' Michael walked slowly round the desk. 'Is that something you brought back with you from Japan?'

She nodded, holding out her arms and allowing him full view of the embroidery on the kimono. 'It had to be made specially, I'm much taller than the average Japanese.'

'Did the Embassy ever recover from your period of employment?'

She glared. 'You are a wretch, Michael. I'll have you know that I left of my own accord after two years exemplary service! They even begged me to stay on.'

'That's why I can't really understand why you're willing to hold the fort here.' Michael looked at her consideringly. 'Leave that, I'll do it,' he said as she reached for the tray. He walked to the door and opened it for her. 'Good night, Red, and thank you for coming. I appreciate it.'

She gave a soft laugh as she moved towards him, a fleeting thought striking her that Michael was one of the few men she was able to physically look up to. 'Oh, what impeccable manners you have! I'm a stick of unlighted dynamite where you're concerned.'

'This time it's you who misjudges me. I'm quite sincere.' He gave a tight smile. 'I know you're not doing this for me, and I'm thanking you on behalf of the children, who very quickly will take you for granted. I want to put it on record that I won't.'

She gave him an uncertain smile as she made her way to the stairs and gained the first tread.

'Have you heard from Kit lately?' Michael asked.

She turned her head, her hair tumbling untidily across her cheek, and said cheerfully: 'He's written a few times, but you know Kit, a terrible correspondent—comes of dealing with words every working day, I imagine. I shall have to shake him up now I'm back.' She allowed her gaze to move lovingly over the hallway and smoothed her hand along the shining wood bannister. 'I adore this house. I always have. It's so solid and durable.' She swept him a warm smile and giving an airy wave of the hand said: 'Good night, Michael,' and made her way up the stairs, her head full of memories. As she turned the bend she looked back.

Michael was still standing in the doorway, watching her, a thoughtful look on his face. He said: 'Sleep well, Red,' and stayed motionless until she was out of sight.

CHAPTER TWO

NICOLA opened the kitchen door, exclaiming: 'Mmm . . . that smells good. 'Morning, Victor.'

Victor Rudd, fifty-ish, small and thin, with a lugubrious face, the pivot around which the Dalmain household was run, cast a glance over his shoulder and then returned his attention to the pan on the stove. He said: 'Things always happen on my day off. What are you doing here, Nicola? I thought you were hobnobbing with the Yanks?'

'I was, Victor dear, but I'm here now, drooling over that crispy bacon.'

'You shall have some as soon as the guv'nor's had his. He's due at the County Court early.' Victor was deftly setting a tray and watching him with growing amusement, Nicola asked:

'Does Michael have his breakfast in bed, Victor?' and he shot her a scandalised look.

'Of course not! He has it in his office. I tell him he'll ruin his digestion working and eating at the same time.' He poked his head at the coffee pot. 'Help yourself.'

'Thanks.' Nicola did so. 'Miss Golding has gone to her sick mother, and isn't coming back.'

'Thank the good Lord for that,' her companion announced, cracking an egg into the pan.

'I'm taking her place.'

Victor's mournful eyes widened. 'Really! Well, I suppose anyone would be better than that woman.'

'Thank you,' replied Nicola mildly. 'The guv'nor was pleased to accept my help.'

'A drowning man will clutch at a straw,' Victor observed as he lifted the tray and walked out, leaving Nicola grinning to herself. She loved Victor and his gloriously sad demeanour and his wealth of prophesies and sayings. He was a bit of a mystery man. It was suspected by most people that Michael had helped him in some way. Inquisitive probings brought no results. Whatever had happened had instilled a fierce loyalty to Michael and his family in Victor ever since, which he hid in a disparaging manner.

The door was flung open and Cassandra swept in, grumbling: 'Why does Michael get preference? I'm starving.'

'Because he pays the bills. Good morning, Cass.'

'Hi, Nickie.' Cassandra dropped her cousin a kiss in passing. 'Do you think I'm getting fat?' she asked. Remembering what it was like being fourteen and the tallest girl in the school, Nicola gave this question the consideration it deserved.

'No, but it does no harm to watch what you eat. Who says you are? Coffee or tea? There's both.'

'Tea, please. Noel did. Brother's are pigs sometimes.'

'Noel isn't usually so insensitive. Anyway, you're still growing.'

'Ye gods! I'm five-five already, I don't want to grow any more!' Cassandra stopped and blushed crimson. 'Oh, lor' Nickie darling, I didn't mean . . .'

'Not to worry, child. The genes that made me tall are not in you.'

'It suits you, Nickie, and you're lovely and slim . . . I mean, you've even done some modelling . . . and I love that track-suit, it's smashing.'

'Thanks, Cass, don't over do it.'

Cassandra grinned. 'No. really, I mean it.' She blew out a deep sigh. 'Am I glad you've come! I desperately need some new clothes and Aunt Margaret was going to take me to Town and her sense of style is positively archaic! Now you can take me instead,' and she beamed happily. Nicola hid a smile. Margaret Dalmain, Kit's mother, was a woman of strong views who aired them frequently.

'Only if Aunt Margaret agrees,' replied Nicola and Cassandra pulled a face and then brightened.

'Michael can deal with Aunt Margaret—he's good at it.' She plonked herself down on a chair and opened up a text book, muttering: 'Filthy French verbs.'

'If you want to be a vet you've got to pass exams,' Nicola pointed out, giving her cup a refill.

'Huh! Can't imagine I'll need to speak French to a cow!' exclaimed Cassandra, head still down, and Nicola smiled, gazing at her young cousin with affection. She was striking to look at, having a mass of marmalade hair, a freckled skin and a large pair of dark spectacles that gave her an owlish appearance. It was her brother, Noel, now walking in, who had inherited the coveted dark auburn hair. He was a good-looking lad whose usually pleasant features were marred today by a gloomy expression. He said an unenthusiastic 'good morning' and flopped down at the table, opening an exercise book.

'A laugh a minute in here,' remarked Victor, coming back in and eyeing the brother and sister. 'I nearly came up the apples and pears to see what was keeping you two. You'll be late if you don't watch it.' He began to dish out food on to plates.

'It's time the guv'nor took a trouble and strife and then perhaps she'd be able to make you get up in time to chew your food properly.'

Cassandra lifted her head and gave him a look of horror. 'Michael? A wife? You've got to be joking, Victor! He's not . . . he hasn't . . .' Words failed her.

An extraordinary feeling of surprise swept over Nicola and she asked: 'Is there someone in the offing, Victor?'

'I'm just saying as it's time he had one, that's all,' Victor answered a little petulantly.

'You've been looking at his palm!' accused Cassandra and Victor shot her a hurt look.

'Now you know the guv'nor won't let me read the future . . .'

'You must *see* the future, Victor, even if you don't tell it,' persisted Cassandra.

Victor slid the plates across the wooden table. 'Maybe, maybe not, but he's sure to have a wife some time, isn't he? A man like him isn't going to stay on his own forever, is he?' He swept them all a pitying glance. 'Nothing stays the same. You must have given the idea some thought.'

'If we have we've pushed it into the background,' acknowledged Noel. 'I suppose he will get landed one of these days. There's that blonde barrister who shares his Chambers. Her father's a judge. I reckon she's got her eye on him.'

Cassandra groaned. 'The awful Geraldine, you mean? She patronises like mad! Oh, I do hope he chooses someone nice.'

'You'll have no say in the matter,' rebuked Victor, 'and keep your eye on the dickory dock or you'll miss the bus,' and picking up the coffee pot he went out.

'Perhaps Michael will be easier to live with if he had a wife,' Noel said, stabbing a piece of bacon on his plate.

'What's the matter, Noel?' asked Nicola quietly, unable to let this pass without making some comment, and Noel shrugged and Cassandra retorted:

'Michael's all right. He's not so stuffy as some of my friends' parents.'

'Not to you, perhaps,' grumbled Noel. 'He can be pretty foul to me.'

'Ah, come on, Noel, that's not fair,' protested his sister. 'You can't blame him for not letting you drive the Cabriolet, especially after the bent wing on the Ford.'

'Anyone could've done that,' flashed back Noel and while they argued the door opened and Michael strolled in. He was wearing a charcoal grey suit with a waistcoat, a striped grey-and-white shirt and a canary yellow tie. Nicola decided that his tall, rangy frame was the perfect foil for good tailoring although he seemed unaware of his clothes once he was wearing them.

He drawled: 'Good morning, everyone. It's a beautiful September day—shouldn't you two be out in it?' He surveyed his half-brother and sister, who had stopped arguing on his entrance, and continued pointedly: 'Miss Golding is not coming back. Nicola is holding the fort for the time being.'

Cassandra gave a whoop of joy and threw her arms, first round Nicola, and then her half-brother, and even Noel's face brightened.

'I have the deepest sympathy with Miss Golding,' Michael went on repressively. 'What are you going to do with the bat, Cassandra?'

'It's all arranged,' she proclaimed in an injured tone. 'Mr Harlow is going to look after it.'

'Hum.' Michael looked at his sister hard and decided not to take the matter further. He turned to his brother. 'You can have the Ford tonight, Noel, if you're going to the Squash Club,' and Noel mumbled his thanks, catching up his books and leaving the kitchen, not meeting anyone's eyes.

Cassandra grabbed a piece of toast and hurriedly followed, turning at the door to say, 'That advert's on the telly again, Nickie—the one in the balloon! All my friend's have watched it!' and then she was gone, shouting goodbye over her shoulder.

'We couldn't find anyone else, they were all afraid of heights,' confessed Nicola apologetically, 'at least, that's not totally right. We found a girl who said she thought she'd be all right and I went with her to hold her hand, so to speak, and she funked it at the last minute.'

'Heights have never bothered you,' stated Michael heavily and Nicola began to smile, recalling numerous escapades of a climbing nature from their past. Deeming it time to change the subject, she remarked:

'Do you think studying is getting Noel down?'

Michael grimaced. 'I very much doubt it. He's a lazy beggar at the best of times. He has a brain but doesn't seem motivated into using it.' He looked at her without speaking and she asked cautiously:

'What's the matter, Michael?'

'I'm getting used to the idea of you being here,' he replied lightly, 'and trying to remember when last you stayed.'

'That might be a little difficult for you,' Nicola

told him. 'When I've visited over the past few years, more often than not, your absence has been conspicuous. Was that intentional?'

'You know I divide my time between here and London, and you've been out of the country a great deal, haven't you? Japan, India and recently America.' With hands in his pockets, Michael leaned back against the Welsh Dresser. 'I can't believe you missed me,' he drawled, his voice amused.

She said flippantly: 'I like to practise the cutting word and the razor edge comment and you're a good opponent.'

'What a pity you've promised to behave.'

'I shan't agree with everything you say!' rebuked Nicola. 'It's not good for you,' and was rewarded by a slow, deepening smile and she found she was smiling back.

'So you're into big business, now, Red?' Michael asked in the ensuing pause and Nicola nodded.

'I hope it's going to be big, eventually. Word is getting about that we're reliable. I've gone into partnership with Jennie Lambert. We met in India. She was with a group of students in a clapped-out van which had broken down and I'd just missed the only bus that week and we got talking. We haven't stopped since. She married one of the students, Bill Lambert, and Jennie and I decided to try our hand at an Agency.' She grinned. '*Angels*. You know, Angels of Mercy and all that jazz. We find things for people, and people for people. The employment side is relatively easy, the search side can be complicated, but fun. Luckily we're building up some good contacts in television and our reputation is growing steadily. Jennie is based at the office and organises the work from there which leaves me time ...' She stopped short and stared absently down at her coffee cup which she then drained, grimacing as the nearly cold liquid slipped down her throat. '... to tout for business.' She carried the cup to the sink. 'Have you much work for me today? I could do with going to Town to fetch my things.'

'There's nothing urgent today. I'm going in around eleven-thirty, you can come with me. I usually take the car to the station and go by train but if you're bringing luggage back with you I'll motor all the way.' Michael glanced at his watch. 'Can you meet me outside the County Court about then? The back entrance by the car-park.' He fell silent for a moment. 'While you're here, Red, do you think you can try and find out what's the matter with Noel? He might talk to you.' He reached the door, pausing to say over his shoulder: 'I like the outfit,' and then was gone.

Nicola sat with her face cupped in her palms, a thoughtful expression descending on her usually animated features.

'Some folk might have nothing to do,' announced Victor, entering, 'but I've got to make a Kate and Sydney, so you'll oblige me by getting off your backside,' and he looked pointedly at the door.

'In a minute,' promised Nicola, liking the sound of Victor's celebrated steak and kidney pie. 'I want to talk. Does Mrs Vesty still come in to clean?'

'That she does, but she doesn't touch my kitchen.'

'If Michael has a secretary at Chambers, which he must have,' mused Nicola, 'then it's only the work he brings home that's done here ...'

'He has a large practice in the county,' broke in Victor.

'. . . plus keeping an eye on the children, which can't be difficult now they're older. Hardly hard work, is it? Come on, Victor, give! Why don't they stay, these secretaries of his?'

Victor grunted and began to stack pots in the bowl. 'There's a number of reasons. We're a bit cut off here for some—we're on a bus route but the buses are few, and although the guv'nor tries for the motherly sort, appearances can be deceiving. They all seem to get ideas in their heads about him—some wanting to mother him as well as the children, which drives him wild, as you can well imagine! And then some . . .'

'Fall for him,' suggested Nicola obligingly, and Victor nodded.

'Like I say, he ought to take a trouble and strife and that would solve things—at least, I hope it would.'

'Is there someone, Victor?'

He grinned. 'Well, not as I know what goes on in London, but he isn't short of a bit of skirt, that I can say, not the guv'nor, but he keeps his private life to himself, see? Still, he's of an age to get cash and carried, and his career's doing all right.' He came to collect more dirty pots from the table. 'He'll do as he likes, as always, and so long as they all stay out of my kitchen . . .'

Nicola said soothingly: 'I'm going.' She lazily stretched and Victor regarded her mournfully. 'What about you, Nicola? When are you going to get yourself an Old Pot and Pan?'

'Old Pot and Pan?' echoed Nicola, thinking she would have to brush up on her rhyming slang. 'Oh! An old man—a husband! Old Pots and Pans aren't the "in" thing these days, Victor.'

'Huh. Can I have a go at your hands soon?'

'So long as you keep your prophesies to yourself,' asserted Nicola, scraping back her chair as she stood up. 'Do you still have sessions, Victor?'

'By invitation only. The guv'nor doesn't mind. Just so as I keep off the future with the family.'

'So I should think,' said Nicola, giving a shiver. Hands, tea leaves or tarot, Victor did the lot, when he was in the right mood. 'The guv'nor's taking me to Town. Could you be a dear and run me to the County Court?' She reached the door and paused for his answer. Victor nodded his assent and then made a big show of eyeing her up and down. 'None of the others ever wore stuff like that.' He sniffed. 'What with the guv'nor's ties and now you—I shall have to start wearing dark glasses in a morning!'

The track-suit was lemon and apple green. Nicola blew him a kiss and made her exit, laughing. She was still smiling as she rang Dalmains and asked to be put through to Mr Christopher Dalmain and gave her name. After a few seconds Kit's voice came on the other end.

'Good lord! Is that really you, Nick?'

Her smile deepened, colouring her voice. 'Yes, it's really me. I'm back.'

'Why didn't you tell me you were coming? I'd've met you in.'

'I thought I'd surprise you. I'm at Bredon House, I'll explain why when I see you. I'm coming to Town today with Michael—any chance of you having lunch with me?'

'Hold on a minute, I'll see.' Kit's voice went away, returning to say: 'Yes, I can wangle it. One o'clock, Ziegfelds. Bring Mike along too. I may have someone with me you'll both be interested to meet.'

'Oh, but Kit, couldn't we . . .?' Nicola was torn between exasperation and amusement. 'Kit, who . . .?'

He laughed. 'No, I want to surprise you. See you both at one,' and he put down the telephone before she could protest any more. Nicola murmured: 'Wretch.' This first meeting with Kit, after so long, was going to be spoiled. She had some funny stories to tell, in tune with his sense of humour and they had a lot to catch up on. She shrugged her shoulders philosophically. Kit at thirty-two still had the capacity for fun that he had at thirteen, when his catch phrase was: 'Hey, do you want a surprise?' He hadn't changed.

The doorman at the County Court informed Nicola that Mr Dalmain was on his way down and if she would like to wait in the car it was unlocked. Nicola thanked him and made her way to the white Jaguar Cabriolet, beautifully sleek and classy. When Michael slid into the driver's seat a few minutes later she said teasingly: 'You always did have good taste in cars, Michael,' and her eyes swept round the walnut trim and leather upholstery.

'The hat's a winner, too,' remarked Michael. 'I've gone up a notch in the doorman's estimation.'

'Only one?' quizzed Nicolá, pleased. Compliments from Michael were a novelty and in consequence meant more. She pulled off the dark green Garbo-type hat and unbuttoned the green and blue tartan cape, tossing the one negligently into the luggage space at the back and hitching the other over her seat. She smoothed the matching green skirt over her knees and settled herself comfortably for the journey ahead, enjoying the speed as the Jaguar zipped along the motorway. Remembering the conversation at the breakfast table, she suddenly exclaimed, 'My goodness, Michael, Noel didn't expect to be allowed to drive *this*?'

Michael replied dryly: 'I soon disabused him of the idea.' He drove some miles in silence and then asked: 'Anything happened I should know of?'

Nicola ticked the items off with a leather gloved finger. 'Two telephone messages, names and numbers noted. Mrs Vesty arrived to "do" the upstairs—Mr Vesty's got a swelling, her Jean's pregnant, twins expected, and our Jack's been in trouble with the police and did I think Mr Dalmain would tell her what to do. The logs have been delivered. I dropped the bat off at the vet's as per instructions by Cass and Mr Harlow thinks it will probably die, but I shan't tell Cass that.'

'If she wants to specialise in animals then she'll have to face up to reality.'

'But it might live,' pointed out Nicola reasonably. 'Oh, yes—what are you doing for lunch?'

'Treating you, I was hoping.'

'What a nice idea! Thank you, but Kit's beaten you to it, and he wants you to come along. One o'clock at Ziegfelds. He has someone he wants us to meet.'

Michael waited until he had overtaken a lorry and then said: 'Ziegfelds it is, then.'

She turned slightly in her seat, her eyes on his face. 'Someone we'll be *surprised* to meet. Any idea who it might be?'

'How should I know, Red?' He glanced at her briefly. 'We'll be surprised together, mmm . . .?'

The headwaiter greeted them at Ziegfelds with just the right amount of deference. 'Mr Dalmain, a pleasure to see you, sir, Mr Christopher Dalmain is in the far corner. Miss Redford, we haven't seen you for some months. Welcome back.'

'Thank you, Logan,' Nicola replied, smiling, and as they were shown to their table, murmured 'What a memory that man has.'

Michael replied: 'Kit will have told him who to expect.'

She pulled a face, muttering: 'You're a rotten cynic!' and then Kit was coming forward to greet them. Kit, unchanged, eyes and mouth laughing, hair shining golden under the amber lights. He flung his arms round Nicola enthusiastically and kissed her.

'Nick, you're looking marvellous! It *is* good to see you!' His eyes looked her up and down with approval. 'That's a darling of a hat, don't you agree, Mike?' He turned to his cousin and shook him warmly by the hand.

They didn't look like cousins at first glance, the one fair-haired, brown-eyed and the other dark with blue eyes. Michael was slightly taller and leaner than Kit, but after a while, these differences became less noticeable and the Dalmain nose and jawline more apparent. There was a strong bond between the two men beyond sharing the same blood and environment and there was no mistaking the genuine affection each held for the other. Kit's greeting, as was to be expected, was ebullient; Michael's much more restrained but his eyes crinkled the way they did and his smile was full of amused affection for his extrovert cousin.

Their greeting over, Kit turned to the person sitting patiently in the corner and in a voice laden with mischief, said 'Now! Guess who this is!'

Before anyone could speak, pouting prettily, the woman protested 'Really, Kit, that's most unfair! We haven't met for years and I hope I've changed since childhood!'

Michael saved Nicola the acute embarrassment of admitting her ignorance by stepping forward, smiling, holding out his hand across the table.

'Hello, Hester . . . I had heard you were back so have an advantage over Nicola.' He glanced over his shoulder. 'You remember Hester Keynes, Red?' and Nicola blinked and gave a gasp of a laugh.

'Hester! My goodness, it *is* a long time, isn't it?' while thinking Hester Keynes! Where on earth has Kit dug her up from? The two women gave a token handshake and Nicola accepted the seat Kit was holding out for her. As the men took their places, Hester's lips formed an amused curve. She turned to Nicola.

'I recognised you immediately, Nicola, even though I was expecting you. You were such a tall, lanky thing as a child . . .'

'Not quite so lanky now,' broke in Kit, giving Nicola a wink.

'. . . you must be all of six feet, surely?'

'Five ten,' offered Nicola and smiled, on her guard. Hester Keynes had, in fact, not altered— she was still as friendly as a snake in the grass.

'What brings you to England, Hester?' Michael asked, passing the menu to Nicola.

While Nicola scanned it, Hester was obliging with, 'Daddy's decided to open up Tadwell this winter and do some entertaining, and he needs me to hostess for him. We shall be having some interesting house-parties, you must come and stay. I've been hearing all kinds of wonderful praise from Daddy about you, Michael.'

'That's very kind of Chapman,' returned Michael pleasantly. 'Shall we order?'

Conversation during the meal was fairly general, although Nicola took a backseat. She watched Hester with growing amusement as Hester asked all the right questions, the wide-eyed listening look and the pretty pouting one vying with each other for top marks.

Hester had never been a close friend of Nicola's when they were children and Nicola's memories were mostly of a pretty, petite little girl, very feminine in frills and flounces, who was always a winner with the adults because of her good behaviour and obedience, but whose petulant tears and tale-bearing habits ostracised her from the rest of the girls in the neighbourhood. Nicola had no time for Hester, who would be adoring and sweetly helpless in the company of Kit and Michael. She was frequently dropped into trouble by one of Hester's innocent-sounding remarks addressed to Aunt Margaret, who in turn complained to her sister-in-law that Nicola was being allowed to run wild and was a bad influence. Auntie Joan was obliged to remonstrate, though mildly, but Uncle John encouraged her, saying to his wife that if Nicola wanted to be one of the boys, let her . . . she'd soon grow into a girl fast enough when the time came.

The two girls' paths diverged in their early teens and looking at her now, an assured, beautiful woman, Nicola was prepared to give her the benefit of the doubt, but didn't hold out much hope that Hester had changed greatly. Hester had been pampered and spoiled all her life and was still being so, by the look of her. She was the only daughter of Chapman Keynes, a wealthy industrialist. Her mother had died ten years previously and Chapman had built a new wing at the Ashwell General hospital in Vera Chapman's honour. Hester's name had been linked in the past with an Italian Count and an American politician, Nicola remembered, but there were no rings on her marriage finger, although there was an abundance on the rest.

No, she hadn't changed much, Nicola thought, watching Hester flutter her lashes, yet there was nothing stupid or empty-headed about her—how could there be, a daughter of Chapman Keynes? The cool grey eyes rested upon Nicola every now and again and although the dark red mouth smiled and the voice was friendly, Nicola was not fooled. She was interested in the men's reactions. Michael was being his usual urbane self, helping the conversation along, while Kit was enjoying himself, filling their wine glasses regularly and slipping in outrageous quips making them all laugh. At one point he turned to Nicola, saying:

'Now you're back, Nick, you'll be able to come to the parents' Ruby Wedding Anniversary.'

'How are they?' Nicola asked.

'Fine, but mother is already getting steamed up about it. You know what she's like—everything must be just so,' he replied, raising his eyes expressively and Nicola chuckled, murmuring that she did indeed!

As they made their way out of the restaurant Hester said, 'Kit tells me you'll be at Bredon

House for a while . . . quite like old times.'

Nicola made a non-committal reply and after arranging with Michael that she would see him at his Chambers later with her luggage, she said her goodbyes and walked round to Angels' office. It was a lovely September afternoon and it was good being back in London. Charing Cross Road was as busy as usual and as she passed Foyles, Nicola thought ahead to when *Code Name Fox* would be out and on the shelves in the bookshops. She hugged the thought enthusiastically. *Code Name Fox* by N. A. Merchant! Merchant was her mother's maiden name and the N. A. was for Nicola Adele, so although she was using a pseudonym it wasn't a name totally unconnected with her.

She turned down a labyrinth of side streets and then stopped at a glossy white-painted door with 'Angels' painted on it in gold. She pushed the door open and climbed the narrow stairs and entered the reception office. She introduced herself to the girl there, new since her trip to the States, and was told to go on in to Jennie's office.

Jennie, small and plump, with a mop of short fair curly hair was talking on the telephone. She waved a welcoming hand and mouthed that she wouldn't be long. Nicola smiled and nodded and sank into a chair. She threw off her cape and undid another button at the neck of her navy blouse, and contemplated the tip of her navy shoe. She was feeling curiously flat. She shouldn't have drunk all that wine, alcohol at mid-day always put her to sleep, and right on cue she gave a large yawn, and smothered a giggle. Fancy seeing Hester after all these years! she thought, and began to look back on her life, a bleak feeling spreading over her. She suddenly felt tired of all the dashing about she'd done and the thought of hibernating at Bredon House was soothing. Still, she'd got *Code Name Fox* out of her stay in Japan, and the new one, *Fox On The Rocks* was set in New York, which she had explored avidly during her stay with Adele and Neil. She was only half-way through it and really needed to shut herself away to finish it, but she couldn't have resisted the appeal in Cassandra's cry for help. It was also strangely appealing to be doing a favour for Michael! She remembered the conversation at breakfast, Victor's claim that Michael should marry, and wondered what this Geraldine person was like.

'. . . decided to take you up on your offer?'

Nicola came in on the tail end of Jennie's question and realised that the 'phone call was over. She pulled a wry face.

'Sorry, Jennie, what was that?'

'Has your cousin decided to take you up on your offer?' Jennie repeated patiently.

'Michael isn't my cousin,' Nicola retorted automatically, 'and yes, for the time being.'

'You don't talk of Michael as often as you do Kit,' her friend prompted, and Nicola shrugged.

'Michael disapproves of me ninety-nine per cent of the time. He thinks I'm flighty, irresponsible and a nut.'

'Coo . . . he sounds a bore.'

'He's not, really, just that he had too many responsibilities thrust upon him too soon and he thinks I'm one of them. In actual fact, when we were kids he invented the most hair-brain adventures which he tried his damnedest to keep me out of.' She grinned. 'He didn't often succeed. As for now, he's made quite a name for himself in the legal profession and can be very good company when he likes, having an extremely dry, caustic type of wit. We tread warily around each other.'

'Are they alike to look at, Kit and Michael? I've met Kit briefly, if you remember,' said Jennie and Nicola took off her hat and rubbed her scalp pleasurably.

'A bit, facially, but Michael's dark-haired and blue-eyed. They both have brains and are good at their job.' She drew the front of her hair away from her forehead with a finger and leaned back in the chair with a posture that in anyone else might have seemed ungainly, continuing thoughtfully: 'Kit's outgoing, easy to get on with, lazy, funny—a flamboyant ladies man. Michael's more complex, wary of showing his feelings, cynical, probably more responsible than Kit, and keeps his private life exactly that. He could be ruthless, if he felt it to be necessary.' She frowned. 'But then, Kit can be, too.'

'Hum ... these Dalmains sound interesting.' The door opened and the girl from reception came in carrying a tray of tea-things. Jennie smiled, said, 'Thanks, Sally,' and as she went out Sally shot Nicola a curious glance. Jennie poured out the tea and handed her friend a cup. 'Have you told them about the writing yet?' When Nicola shook her head, she persisted, her tone indicating how extraordinary she thought this. 'Not even Kit?'

'Especially Kit!' Nicola took a sip from the cup. 'I shall have to tell him eventually, of course, but in the beginning I couldn't. How embarrassing if he'd turned it down! I was determined *Code Name Fox* was going to stand on its own two feet. Not that Kit would have hesitated in telling me it was no good, if that's what he thought, but I wasn't going to give him the chance.' She gave a chuckle. 'Dalmains think I'm a man and I haven't disillusioned them.'

'N. A. Merchant does sound masculine,' agreed Jennie, refilling her cup, 'and a spy thriller doesn't seem to be the usual woman's genre.' She eyed her friend mischievously. 'Your hero Fox is gorgeous. I can't believe he's a figment of your imagination.'

'If he was real I'd snap him up quick,' quipped Nicola, rising gracefully to her feet and crossing to return her cup to the tray. 'How's business, or shouldn't I ask?'

'Ask away—it's growing steadily. If I'm stuck at any time, can I ring you?'

'So long as I have some notice, yes. I see the balloon advert's on again.'

'There might be a parachute jump coming up soon,' began Jennie doubtfully and Nicola's face brightened.

'Great! If you can't find anyone to do it, ring me.'

Jennie groaned a laugh and then asked, 'Shall you be able to get on with your writing while you're in Surrey?'

'I ought to be able to,' replied Nicola. 'I very nearly let the cat out of the bag this morning to Michael, only just stopped in time.' She brought up her wrist and glanced at her watch. 'I'd better go. Thanks for bringing my cases in with you, Jennie.' She lifted the cape from the chair, hesitated over the hat and decided to hold it, and collected her clutch bag from the table. 'I feel a bit of a fraud, Jennie, about the business. I'm hardly here.'

Jennie came round the desk and gave her friend

a hug. 'Don't be silly. We got it off the ground together and now your writing has taken off it's much better that you should concentrate on that. We're able to afford office help now—leaving me to do the administration. In fact, everything's working out fine.'

Satisfied, Nicola said, 'Keep in touch, you know the number—and give my love to Bill.'

Jennie promised that she would and when Nicola had departed sat at her desk wondering if she could introduce Nicola to the new bod in Bill's department without it looking too much like match-making.

Travelling swiftly along the motorway *en route* home, the two suitcases stacked behind the seats, and the Jaguar making short work of the miles, Nicola asked, 'How on earth did Kit find Hester Keynes?'

Michael said, 'I believe Chapman put some business their way and you know Aunt Margaret, she would issue a dinner invitation to anyone who had graced the front page of *The Times*, even if it was an orang-outang from London Zoo.'

Nicola giggled and sighed. 'Poor Uncle Rupert.'

'Rupert's all right. He lives in a world of books.' Michael paused, taking the turn-off for Ashwell before adding, 'What do you think to Kit's surprise?'

Nicola said calmly, 'Not much,' and then, as if she felt the reply too brief, 'She was a real pain when we were kids—I doubt she's altered.'

Michael gave her a hooded glance and made no comment.

CHAPTER THREE

THE days began to form a pattern. Before a week was out Nicola felt as though she had never been away, so easily did she fit in with life at Bredon House. She loved the odd, irregular shape of the building, its age and quaintness appealed visually although she was quite happy to share the luxury of central heating and other unobtrusive modernising which had been done over the years. Nicola would lean out of her bedroom window and feast her eyes on the garden below. The patch of kitchen garden in the sheltered corner was Victor's plot, which he guarded jealously. The rest, although tended by Mrs Vesty's husband, was not set out in a regimentated manner but was an interesting miscellany of shrubs, hedges and trees, a rough paddock, a mown lawn and at the moment ablaze with the final fling of summer colour—marigolds, asters, flocks, and covering the wall beneath the window a beautiful creamy white clematis.

Nicola had always had a good rapport with her young cousins, Noel and Cassandra. She could see why Michael was uneasy regarding Noel. He was admittedly the quieter of the two children, but seemed to be even more withdrawn and quick to take offence. She probed gently but did not force the issue. If he wanted to talk he would do so eventually.

Cassandra was a delight, and showed how happy she was in having Nicola there by constantly saying so, and showing an avid interest in her clothes and make-up, which Nicola, being blessed with a good complexion, used sparingly but to good effect. She encouraged Cassandra to have her fine, fly-away hair cut and layered and gave her nails a weekly manicure in an endeavour to stop her nibbling them.

Michael was the biggest revelation, however. Since being an adult Nicola had never stayed long in his company other than with the extended family, when he tended to listen more than talk, usually viewing the proceedings with a somewhat jaundiced eye, his sardonic features faintly humorous. As the weeks passed through September and October there was a confirmation of what she had always suspected, that behind that quiet exterior were untold depths, waiting to be discovered. She pitted her wits against him constantly, finding the ensuing crosstalk exhilarating. She found his work interesting and coped easily with it, once she had grown used to the legal jargon. At times she would even score a point in their argument and her barely concealed glee would make Michael smile, one of his lazy, lop-sided varieties, and it was with something of a shock to find how much she liked making him smile.

Nicola was scrupulous in dealing with all Michael's work before her own. She had explained to her cousins that she often did some typing for Angels, her agency, to account for working in the evening, but she made sure not to work if Michael was at home. He was liable to show an interest and she didn't want to prevaricate too much.

She began to build up a dossier of telephone voices—Henry, the head clerk at Chambers, he had a slight West Country burr, Mr Ralston, a solicitor, who had an attractive Scottish accent, and Geraldine Forest, a fellow barrister, who had a pleasant non-regional voice and a friendly enough manner, although Nicola understood Cassandra's complaint of being patronised. Miss Forest, on the telephone at least, was a little superior.

Nicola also met some of Michael's clients. Michael tried to organise his week so that he spent two days dealing with out-of-Town cases and on occasions clients, with their solicitor, would come to Bredon House.

There are a number of adjustments to be made when someone is pitchforked into a household that is already set in its ways. Nicola breezed into the bathroom one morning, expecting it to be empty, for Michael and Noel usually used the downstairs shower-room, and she had heard Cassandra going down the stairs. Michael was standing at the wash-basin, a towel round his neck, wearing white boxer shorts, shaving at the mirror.

Her stride halted at the sight of him and yelping an apology Nicola began to back out.

Michael said calmly, 'Hold on, I've nearly finished,' and with a couple more deft strokes made final pathways into the soap on his chin. He began to rinse the razor under the tap. 'My fault. Noel beat me to the downstairs one and as this was free . . .'

'Be my guest,' Nicola offered, lowering herself on to the edge of the bath and hiding a yawn. ''Fraid I overslept.' She had been working late into the night on her new manuscript and was paying for it now. Absently watching him Nicola thought how deceptive bodies were when they were clothed. Looking at the bare back and limbs she could see that there was a fit man hidden beneath the expensive clothes and the controlled, almost indolent image. 'You're nicely tanned, Michael.'

He glanced at her through the mirror. 'I have friends in France and caught the best of their summer.' He wiped away a blob of shaving soap from his ear and dropped razor, brush and soap into a toilet bag. 'The Dordogne . . . do you know it?'

She shook her head. 'I've heard it's lovely there. Unspoilt.'

'Best out of season, but then, anywhere is.' He smoothed a hand over his jaw critically and satisfied, turned from the mirror.

Nicola gasped, 'Michael! How on earth did you do that?' and Michael glanced down at the faded scar below his rib-cage and tilted her a sardonic look, his voice a drawl.

'That, my dear Red, was a legacy from a memorable bicycle ride when I was seventeen. A spin down Coplow Hill, remember?'

'Of course I remember,' she said, 'but I didn't know you were scarred for life too,' and she pulled back the sleeve of the kimono to reveal a similar scar running down her arm. 'I came off and brought you down as well,' she reminisced cheerfully. 'I was far more concerned and upset about my busted bike than with any injuries. Poor you!' She wrinkled her nose consideringly. 'I wonder why Kit seemed to survive without mishap all the time?'

'Possibly because he steered clear of you.' Michael ran a comb quickly through his hair and dropped it into the bag. 'Sorry about not locking the door. Hope it hasn't done your maidenly modesty too much damage?' and he smiled mockingly, turning to go.

Nicola looked at him askance. 'You've grown some, and the hairs on your chest have multiplied, but don't forget I've seen you swimming in the buff a few times,' she told him challengingly. What the hell did he think she'd been doing the past ten years? Living in a nunnery?

Stopped at the door by this claim, Michael slowly turned, gave her a thorough going over with cool, amused eyes, and drawled, 'Likewise—and the skinny urchin you were then, Red, has much improved,' and he bowed himself out.

Nicola sat on for a few moments, a rueful smile forming on her lips. She had asked for that one. She stood up and viewed herself critically in the mirror. It was quite apparent that she was wearing nothing under the kimono—but she hadn't expected to bump into Michael—and it clung like a second skin. Her eyes fixed absently on the neat fullness of breasts, the flatness of stomach and the rounded sweep of buttocks, moving down the long length of her legs. A ghost of a smile tugged at her mouth. Had she finally managed to make Michael see her as a grown woman at last? Wonders would never cease! Her gaze went back to her face and the yellow-brown eyes stared back accusingly. She broke the mesmeric stare by putting out her tongue and went to lock the door.

Rupert and Margaret Dalmain lived about half a mile away at Holly Lodge and Kit, who had a house in London, made regular sorties to Ashwell and was a frequent visitor to Bredon House on those occasions. He was a popular favourite with his young cousins and would often arrive unexpectedly with an outing or project afoot. He quizzed Nicola about her stay in the States, he knew New York well, and Nicola very nearly admitted to him that she was N. A. Merchant but something held her back, a resolve to keep to her original intention of seeing how *Code Name Fox* was received. She hugged the thought of his surprised face, when she finally told him, to herself with glee, imagining Kit's amazement. Michael's reaction she didn't dwell on, because it was difficult to imagine. He had bookshelves full of legal tomes in his office, and a huge floor-to-ceiling shelf unit in his bedroom which housed mostly classics and some more modern writers. She couldn't be compared to Hemingway, Forster, Bates or Lee, but they were sitting side by side with Tom Sharpe and Dick Francis, so there was hope for her yet.

Nicola and Kit had slipped back into their easy, teasing relationship, enjoying each other's company. Driving back from an evening in London Kit teasingly broke a companionable silence.

'Had any rows with Mike recently?' The glance he gave her before returning his attention to the road ahead was full of fun.

'Michael and I,' proclaimed Nicola loftily, 'are on our best behaviour.'

'Are you?' Kit gave a laugh. 'That I can't believe.'

Nicola grinned. 'It's true, nevertheless. Nearly eight weeks and we haven't had a row!'

'Ah, well,' Kit said, 'it suits Mike having you at Bredon, doesn't it? It pays him to make an effort. I wonder if the strain will prove too much for the poor old chap?'

A stab of unease struck Nicola and she gazed at Kit uncertainly. Was that the reason she was getting on so well with Michael? A deliberate policy on his part? The thought was slightly deflating. She gave herself a mental shake and said cheerfully, 'Works both ways. He's doing me a favour too—and you never really know with Michael, do you? He doesn't give much away.'

Kit nodded agreement, driving the Mustang expertly round the twisting country lanes. 'Remember when Mike switched to law and didn't tell anyone until it was done?' Kit asked. 'He just waited patiently for the furore to blow over. Uncle John was upset and I must admit, I was too. I was looking forward to Mike being in with me when the old-'uns retired.' The headlights picked up the sign to Ashwell and Kit turned to follow its direction and soon the familiar landmarks came into sight and he slowed to a halt at the entrance to the drive.

'Are you coming in for coffee?' Nicola asked and Kit shook his head, squinting at the dash clock.

'No. I must resist the temptation.' He put his arm round her shoulder as they leisurely walked up the drive.

'Thank you for a lovely evening, Kit, I did enjoy the play,' Nicola said, staring up at the stars, thinking winter's here, there's a definite chill in the air, and shivered slightly.

'Me to.' Kit must have felt the shiver. He stopped and moved her round so that he could see her face in the moonlight and folded his other arm round her. 'It's good to have you back, Nick,' he said, and before she could say anything in reply he kissed her. It was a long kiss with a strange urgency underlying it.

Catching her breath, laughing a little, Nicola murmured, 'I'm glad you missed me.' She looked into his face, suddenly unsure of his mood and went on lightly, 'Was that for any particular reason?' She hesitated, 'Is anything wrong, Kit?'

'Lord, no!' He grinned, teeth gleaming whitely, and hugged her to him. 'Do I have to have a reason?' he demanded whimsically. He glanced at the house, at the cracks of light escaping the curtains in one of the downstairs windows. 'I'm not sure I approve of this truce with Mike—don't get too friendly with him, will you?'

'Kit!' protested Nicola, and felt the colour rush to her cheeks. 'Don't be stupid! No-one will ever take your place, you know that! You can hardly begrudge Michael a little civility and co-operation.' She searched his face uncertainly.

Kit laughed, his brown eyes quizzing her. 'I must be jealous.' He smoothed a finger across her furrowed brow. 'I guess I've got used to you two being daggers drawn and me being the mediator in the middle—and now find myself out of a job.'

Relieved by the wry amusement in his voice Nicola grinned. 'Not for long,' she prophesied. 'I can't see this calm lasting, can you?'

He kissed the end of her nose. 'Not really, but—wonders will never cease!'

'Miracles do happen!'

'A lull before the storm!'

Nicola wracked her brains, laughed, and cried triumphantly 'One good turn . . .'

'Make hay while the sun shines!' Kit waited, eyes dancing and Nicola laughed and shook her head. This throwing proverbs and sayings back and forth like ping-pong balls was a relic of their youth. 'I give in—it's too late, I can't think . . . I'm out of practise, that's the trouble.' She shivered again.

'You'd better go in.' He kissed the end of her nose. 'Take care, Nick. I'll give you a call.'

Nicola paused in the doorway and watched him go down the drive, her face thoughtful. More than Kit's surprising behaviour was the realisation that she did not want the truce with Michael to end. She had joked with Kit because that was what was expected of her, but she was getting used to this new friendship of theirs and was fiercely resentful of any threat to it. As she closed the front door behind her Michael appeared in the sitting-room doorway.

'Will you come in and join us for coffee, Nicola?' He stood aside for her to enter. 'This is Geraldine Forest, a colleague of mine. Geraldine, you remember me mentioning Nicola Redford, my cousin, who has stepped so nobly into the breach here?'

Not betraying the use of the word 'cousin' by so much as a flicker of the eye, Nicola smiled at the woman and moved forward to take her outstretched hand. About thirty-five, good figure, blonde hair framing an intelligent face, smart suit, Italian shoes, looking more feminine than the brisk, organising voice on the other end of the telephone led one to suspect.

'How do you do, Miss Redford? How nice to have a face to link with the voice.'

Nicola made an appropriate answer and accepted a cup of coffee from Michael. The 'cousin' bit had thrown her into a strange panic. Michael had never claimed cousinship with her before—why now? The only reason she could think of was to put Geraldine's mind at rest—cousins were no threat.

Nicola left them as soon as she reasonably

could. Geraldine was staying the night. As Nicola passed the guest bedroom she wondered if Geraldine was going to occupy it alone, and then shrugged her shoulders impatiently as she climbed the further set of stairs to her own bedroom, high-up in the gable end of the house . . . what business was it of hers?

In the morning Nicola hung back and allowed Geraldine the use of the upstairs bathroom first, and when she finally arrived down stairs found that Cassandra was giving their guest the 'white mouse test'. From the look of things Geraldine was passing with flying colours and was even encouraging one to crawl along her arm. Nicola bit her lip to stop herself smiling at the look of disappointment on Cassandra's face. Breakfast was set in the dining room, making the start of the day alien and as Michael drove down the drive, Geraldine smiling at him, Victor commented, 'That's the third time she's stayed over. Must be running favourite.'

Fox on the Rocks, the second Fox adventure, was progressing. Nicola was able to arrange her time so that she could spend some of it working on the manuscript. Two letters arrived for Nicola that day. One from her mother of which the final paragraph asked if she was well and happy? Nicola stood at her bedroom window, letter in hand, staring out of the window, eyes fixed un-seeingly on the spread of farmland beyond the boundary hedge with a herd of cows in one of the fields and crows calling from a nearby wood. Yes, she was well . . . and of course she was happy, but there was an odd unsettled feeling not far beneath the surface, as if, for once, she was unsure of both herself and the future.

The other letter, forwarded by Jennie from her home address, was from Dalmains, informing N. A. Merchant that *Code Name Fox* would be in the bookshops on the second day of December. A thrill of anticipation shot through Nicola on reading this, seeing in her mind's eye her book displayed in the shops.

November, always a slightly depressing month, lived up to its reputation and was, for the most part, damp and grey with low-lying mists hanging over the countryside in the mornings and the hint of colder weather to come at night.

In order to be independent Nicola had bought a second-hand VW Beetle, sprayed a bright orange, and was driving home from a trip to Ashwell for more typing paper when she saw Cassandra waving madly from the grass verge about half a mile from Bredon House. She pulled to a stop and Cassandra ran across the road, Nicola wound down the window.

'Someone's thrown a sack in the river, Nickie—do come and see if you can get it ... I mean, it might be anything, mightn't it?' Her anxious face peered through the window.

'Cass! You've not tried to get it yourself!' Nicola swung out of the car and groaned as she saw Cassandra's legs, covered in mud. Her cousin shook her head violently.

'No, Nickie, honestly! Do come,' and she tugged at Nicola's coat and giving a smothered sigh Nicola switched off the engine, banged the door shut and they stumbled their way across the rough grass leading down to the river.

'Michael will murder you if he finds out you've been near this bloody river!'

'Honest to God, Nickie, I just went to investigate but with all the rain we've had the ground's all boggy on the bank. You see, I'd just got off the school bus and was going home by the field way because I wanted to have a look at the old oast-house. Mr Harlow reckons that the bats are probably nesting in it and it wasn't far from where I found the baby-bat. Anyway, I'd just climbed the stile when I saw this chap throw a sack into the river and run off. Well! I couldn't just ignore it, could I?' and Cassandra turned an indignant face.

'Being who you are, Cass, no, you couldn't.' She stopped as they reached the bank and surveyed the swollen river uneasily. 'Where is it?'

'There,' said Cassandra, pointing towards the bridge. After all the rain the river was running swiftly and the usual debris was being brought along on the surface, some being caught and held at the point where the centre span of the bridge divided the river. The sack was half in the water, caught on the broken limb of a tree. Nicola said:
'It's probably only rubbish, Cass,' and right on cue the sack gave a twitch and from it's depths came a forlorn whimper.

'It's an animal!' whispered Cassandra, horrified. 'Oh, Nickie, it'll drown!' and she took a couple of paces down the bank until Nicola grabbed her arm, saying firmly:

'Don't you dare do anything stupid!' She thought for a moment, weighing up the odds and then said: 'Here, hold my coat.'

'What are you going to do?' Cassandra took the coat and looked at her cousin anxiously, her concern switching rapidly from the sack to Nicola.

'As a child I used to be able to climb down this

bridge when we went fishing. It remains to be seen whether I've still got the touch.' She was talking as she walked to the centre of the bridge, peering over the edge.

'It's beginning to drizzle with rain. It'll make everything slippy,' warned Cassandra, torn in two, but impressed by her cousin's matter-of-fact attitude, and the nonchalant way she swung herself over the parapet. Leaning over she saw Nicola reach the base of the span, to stand precariously on a narrow concrete ledge. 'Can you reach it?' she called down.

'There's a boat-ring set in the stonework,' shouted up Nicola, her voice echoing. 'I'll be able to hang on to that.'

'Do be careful!' Unable to see what was going on, Cassandra ran back to the bank and watched anxiously as Nicola gingerly tested her weight on the branch, hanging on with one hand clutching the boat-ring. 'Oh, don't fall in, Nickie,' Cassandra muttered to herself and froze as Nicola shouted: 'Here goes,' and reached for the sack. The branch gave way, taking Nicola's booted leg with it, but her hand had grasped the neck of the sack and with a super-human effort she swung back, scrabbling in an undignified manner for balance before calling triumphantly: 'Done it.' She edged cautiously round the ledge and shouted: 'It's awfully heavy, Cass. I doubt I'll be able to get it up without help.'

'I'll tie our belts together. Wait a sec'.' A moment later Cassandra let down the rope of belts and Nicola quickly tied the end round the sack, the rest round her waist, calling:

'I'm coming up now. As soon as you can reach, take the strain, but don't, for heaven's sake, fall over the edge.' She made it, not without difficulty, and climbed over the parapet, breathing heavily, muttering: 'I'm getting too old for this sort of thing.' Cassandra attacked the sack with her penknife while Nicola rubbed her hands and knees rather ineffectually with a handkerchief.

'It's a puppy,' exclaimed Cassandra, as she withdrew a bedraggled bundle from the interior of the sack. 'Is it dead?'

Nicola pressed her palm against it's chest. 'No, but it's not far off. Wrap it in my coat and let's get home. The sooner it's dry and warm the better.'

Victor groaned loudly as they walked in. Cassandra said crossly, 'Oh, don't be silly, Victor, we couldn't leave the thing to drown, could we?' and seeing his look of horror when he saw the state Nicola was in she added, suddenly doubtful, 'It wasn't dangerous, was it, Nickie?' and then: 'What will Michael say?'

'Plenty,' said Victor dourly.

'Victor, be a dear and find a box and a blanket for this miserable scrap, like the angel you are,' urged Nicola, 'and Cass, you'd better ring Mr Harlow and ask him to come over. I shouldn't think warm milk will hurt him, do you?' Cassandra disappeared to telephone.

'It's got big paws . . . probably grow into a wolf-hound,' Victor muttered, eyeing the pup suspiciously.

Nicola grinned, rubbing the animal with a towel. 'Cheer up, Victor, you can't fight fate and Cassandra.'

'I knew something horrible was going to happen when I read the tea leaves this morning,' Victor replied. 'Well—I'd like to be around when the guv'nor sees it,' he went on with relish.

Mr Harlow, the vet, arrived after evening surgery and gave the puppy a thorough examination. It was about six months old, he thought, and sadly undernourished. When he asked if they were intending to keep the puppy, Noel, who had arrived from college and been brought up to date, pulled a wry face at Cassandra and replied, 'I'm afraid that depends on my brother.'

Over their evening meal Cassandra announced that the dog's name was Hamlet—she was studying that particular play for 'O' levels.

'To be or not to be,' joked Noel.

They watched television, waiting uneasily for Michael to come home, and then Victor answered the telephone and came in to say that Michael was going to be late. Cassandra wandered disconsolately into the kitchen and gave a bowl of porridge to Hamlet, Nicola followed her.

'I'll wait up for Michael, and tell him about Hamlet.'

Cassandra's face brightened. 'Oh, would you, Nickie?' She looked at the empty bowl. 'Gosh, he soon lapped that up, didn't he? He's looking better already.'

Nicola bathed and donned pyjamas and gown and taking a hot drink into the sitting room curled up in a chair to watch the late film. She woke to find Michael putting another log on the fire and the television switched off. She glanced sleepily at the clock and found it was a quarter to one. 'Hello, Michael,' she murmured and smiled up at him and the remembered why she was waiting for him and sat up, pushing the hair back from her face and rubbing the sleep out of her eyes. Michael, wiped the dirt from the logs off his hands with a handkerchief.

'I should tell you that I have already met the creature in the kitchen. Some waif and stray of yours, or Cassie's, Red?'

'Cass found him, but I had a hand in it, I'm afraid. His name is Hamlet. Can I get you a drink? Tea?'

'I already have something a little stronger, thank you. I have the feeling I'm going to need it,' he replied, taking a sip of liquid from his glass. 'You'd better tell me what happened.'

As the story unfurled it was apparent that Michael was not to be appeased by any of the humour that Nicola was embellishing it with and she changed tactics and finished it off simply as a statement of facts. Michael sat silent for a few moments before saying, with great restraint. 'You do realise how dangerous it was, don't you? The river is in full spate, there's already been a couple of children drowned. If you'd fallen in you could have got into extreme difficulty, and what would Cassandra have done? Gone in after you, without a doubt, and you could both have drowned! I thought I could trust you to keep Cass out of trouble, and find you can't even keep yourself out of it!'

'Oh, stop being so stuffy, Michael! It wasn't as dangerous as all that—not half as bad as some of the things we used to get up to.'

'I grow grey at the memory of them,' Michael retorted coldly. 'All your life you've rushed head-long into things. I had hoped you'd gained some sense with the years. It seems I was mistaken!'

Nicola had envisaged Michael's impatience, possible annoyance, over the fact that they had kept the dog, rather than let Mr Harlow take it away with him, but she had not conceived this bitter anger, this lashing tongue allied to a contemptuous expression. She sensed a curious deadening feeling in the pit of her stomach and allowed the adrenalin to take over, abandoning tact and diplomacy, anger flaring—anything was better than this hopelessly forlorn feeling of rejection and loss. She welcomed the anger. It would never do to let him know the hurt.

'Don't be so bloody-minded, Michael! Am I *never* to live down my childhood for you? You're so damned disapproving, *nothing* I do is right! Do you think I didn't realise what was at risk? I assessed the situation and decided to have a go. Have you thought what would have happened if I hadn't? Cass would have, more than likely, attempted to do so herself!' She caught her breath, going on bitterly: 'I thought we had a better understanding of one another—it seems I was mistaken.' She shot up out of the chair and felt furiously for her slippers with her toes. Thrusting her hair angrily out of her eyes, she shot him a look. 'I'd better go, if that's what you think of me. I'll find you someone to take my place, and then I'll go.' She took a couple of steps before Michael flung out a hand to stay her progress. His face was pale and his eyes, half-hidden by lowered lids darkened.

'Let me go, Michael—we have nothing more to say to each other.'

'I think we have. Running away isn't the answer,' he said bitingly. 'Calm down and listen.'

'Calm down?' she echoed angrily, struggling to get free. 'Isn't that just like you, Michael! Delivering blistering, insulting comments in that glacial, lofty manner of yours, like a bloody judge and then tell me to calm down!' She jerked her wrists again and ground out, '*Will* you let me go, damn it!' She glared at him, eyes flashing topaz, speaking volumes. 'You're hurting me!'

'Then stop fighting me.' Michael wrenched her to him, his arm like a steel band across her back. The kimono had fallen off her shoulders and one strap of the camisole pyjamas slipped over her arm as she was crushed to him, her movement curtailed. 'I have no wish to enact a melodrama.'

Nicola stood taut, sustaining eye contact, and then suddenly she was released and Michael turned away, taking the glass from where he had put it on the mantel and draining it. Nicola gave a scathing: 'Thank you,' and rubbed her wrist where his fingers had dug into the flesh and stared resentfully at his back.

'You're not without perception, Red—you must know it isn't easy being guardian to a young and growing girl and not only for her safety. That child has given me as many nightmares as you used to do . . .'

'I?' Nicola's eyes glowered indignantly. 'I was never your responsibility!'

He swung round and gave a short laugh without a vestige of amusement in it, his face darkening with colour. 'Don't be more infuriating than you already have been, Red. I was the eldest and you were staying with my family—what was I supposed to do, ignore you?'

'You tried hard enough,' she taunted, cheeks flushed, eyes bright and Michael's hand clenched on the mantel, the knuckles showing white. 'You're damned right, I did, but you were so self-destructive that I was forced to do something about you. There's much of you in Cassandra—diluted, maybe, but enough for her heart to rule her head . . .'

'Yours has never done that, I suppose? You're too darned calculating, Michael—you want to be glad Cass has some red blood in her veins and not ice . . .'

'. . . leading her into impossible situations.' Michael stopped, her words overlapping his, the meaning perfectly clear. His face went blank and Nicola had a swift pang of remorse and then remembered that he was being scathing about Cassandra being too much like her, and the hurt overcame the remorse.

'Cass knows she is forbidden near the river unless with an adult. Why you both couldn't have . . .'

'I'm sorry to be such a disappointment to you, Michael,' Nicola broke in bitterly, 'but I've never been very high on your list, have I? And I *am* an adult, damn you! How old do I have to be before you stop treating me like a child?'

There was a heavy silence, broken only by the grandmother clock ticking on the wall and the occasional splutter from a log drying out in the fire. Nicola, glaring into Michael's face saw it change from grim exasperation to sardonic humour.

'Oh, I think I know you're not a child,' he announced repressively, and before she knew what was happening, before she could utter one word of protest, his hands came down on to her shoulders, one gripping the silk of the kimono, the other warm, bare flesh, and she was pulled roughly into his arms and his mouth came down upon hers.

The world turned over. Slowly.

The slap of her palm against his face resounded sharply in the stunned silence. It was a reflex action on Nicola's part which she regretted the minute it was done. She could have wept with mortification. Such a wretchedly silly thing to do, she had always thought, and in this case putting so much more importance to a typical male action proving male dominance, or trying to. But nothing made sense any more.

With a sardonic twist to his mouth, Michael drawled, 'How delightfully feminine of you, Red. You have most admirably proved my point.'

Shaken more by the fact that he had kissed her, like that, than the actual kiss itself, Nicola, finding her tongue, demanded, 'Damn you, Michael, why did you do that?'

'You seemed to be harbouring doubts as to how I saw you. I trust I've dispelled them?' and his eyes flickered over her dishevelled clothing. 'No one, looking at you now, Red, could fail to mistake you for anything but a woman,' and he turned from her, leaning an arm along the mantel, staring down into the fire. Nicola stood like a dummy, rampant with confusion, face bright red, and pulled the kimono round her, tying the belt with trembling fingers. Michael went on, the hint of weary impatience in his voice. 'We'll talk tomorrow when we're both calmer.' He paused. 'If you want to leave, Red, that's up to you.'

Leave? Of course she didn't want to leave! What was the idiot talking about?

She stood irresolute, searching for the right words and Michael said sharply: 'Good night, Red.' Without answering, she left him.

CHAPTER FOUR

'ALL lost your tongues?' questioned Victor the next morning as he brought back Michael's tray. 'The guv'nor wants to see you,' he further announced, poking his head at Cassandra, who shot Hamlet a longing look, pulled a grimacing face at her cousin and brother and departed with dragging feet.

Ten minutes later a subdued Cassandra returned, red-faced and looking as though she had been crying. She crossed the kitchen to the box and picked up Hamlet, cuddling him, receiving in return a furious wagging of his tail.

'What did he say?' asked Noel and Nicola found herself thinking indignantly that if Michael had been horrible she would go in and blast him to blazes!

Cassandra lifted a tremulous face. 'Michael says we can keep him! Isn't that marvellous?' and she kissed the top of Hamlet's curly head.

Victor sniffed. 'I hope you know what you're letting yourself in for, that's all I can say. How did you bring the guv'nor round?'

Wide-eyed, Cassandra replied, 'I didn't, honestly, he just asked me what had happened yesterday, and I told him, and he asked if I wanted to keep Hamlet, and I said yes please, and he said I could, and made a few stipulations, quite reasonable ones, and then I burst into tears.' She beamed. 'I think Michael had already decided—that I could keep him, I mean.' She put the puppy down and as she straightened looked gratefully at her cousin. 'You must have talked him round last night, Nickie. Thank you, you are a dear.'

Nicola shook her head. 'I doubt it,' she murmured, thinking it really was not fair of Michael, doing an about-turn like this.

After a few minutes made hectic by the collecting of lunch packets, school bags and coats, brother and sister left. Nicola sat on, finishing the cup of tea she was drinking, both hands round the cup, face pensive. Victor shot her a sharp look and said:

'Had a row did you?'

'Oh, shut up, Victor,' replied Nicola wearily. For once the house seemed restrictive and she said abruptly: 'I'm going out.' Ignoring his raised brows she used the back door so that there was no possibility of bumping into Michael.

There was a definite nip in the air and she pulled up the collar of her coat, tugging the wool cloche hat snugly over her ears and set off, walking briskly. At the end of the drive she met Mrs Vesty who called cheerfully: 'You're out early, Miss Redford!' Mrs Vesty was always cheerful.

She bustled up and planted herself solidly in front of Nicola who was forced to stop. 'Will it be all right if I do Mr Dalmain's office today? You're looking a bit peaky, m'dear. Hope you're not sickening for something—our Jean's been ever so poorly with a tummy bug that's going round like lightning.'

'I'm fine, Mrs Vesty, thanks,' lied Nicola, 'and I'm afraid Mr Dalmain is home today, but you'll be able to do his office tomorrow.'

'Right you are,' replied Mrs Vesty, and she and

Nicola side-stepped each other and went their separate ways.

Her breath turned white as Nicola climbed the stile, following the footpath over the common. There were not many people about. A couple of joggers in the distance. A man walking his dog.

She had escaped the house, and Michael, to sort out her muddled thoughts. Nicola could appreciate Michael's point of view—it couldn't be easy bringing up Cassandra, or Noel, for that matter. If Cassandra was the type to get into scrapes often, then it was understandable that Michael would be extra sensitive about her. It didn't help that he also had a hang-up about herself, left over from their childhood.

So, where did that leave her? With a dented self-esteem, she admitted wryly. She had become used to this new relationship with Michael and was enjoying the expansion of understanding between them. It was a shock, therefore, to realise on what shaky ground it was built. She was daunted by how desolate, how deprived she felt, knowing she had lost the ground recently won, and all because of a scraggy mongrel.

Yet, if she had to live yesterday again she would probably do exactly the same. She had reached the highest point of the common and turned her steps to the old pavilion, sitting down on the hard wooden seat, her eyes wandering absently over the deserted bandstand and beyond that, the playing fields of her youth. Down below, the road wound its way in the distance, cars and lorries looking as small as children's toys.

But she hadn't come to look at the view, she had escaped to think about that kiss. What on earth had possessed Michael to kiss her like that? It was so out of character, that was the amazing thing. She could still feel the bruising pressure of his hands gripping her arms, feel the hardness of his mouth against hers. Even if Michael had been furious with her, to be kissed in anger was a demoralising form of punishment—and he bloody well deserved that clout, she thought truculently.

She dug her chin lower in the collar of her coat and gave an impatient sigh. The point was, it hadn't been so much a melodrama as a farce!

A noise—a pebble against a shoe, a snap of a twig, something, or perhaps a sixth sense that warns everyone in certain circumstances, made Nicola look up. Michael was standing watching her, wearing his enigmatic mask. For a split second, eyes widening on contact, Nicola was held, mesmerized by that steady, piercing regard, and then she wrenched her gaze away, tightening her lips stubbornly.

In the brief look she had taken everything in about him. The brown polo-necked sweater under the camel coat, the stone coloured cords, the sheepskin gloves, the long, thin mustard and brown scarf Cassandra had diligently knitted hanging over his shoulders, wrapped loosely round once, the tinge of colour the cold air had brought to his cheeks, the rumpled hair, the mobile mouth held firmly in check. All that, in one brief glance and the image stayed with her as she stared, unseeing, out front.

Michael said conversationally, 'Victor told me the direction you'd taken and Mrs Vesty confirmed it, and I thought you'd be here.' He gave a soft laugh. 'Our old headquarters.' He sat down on the seat leaving a gap between them.

The miserable lump that had settled inside her

as a result of their quarrel, that cold core of unhappiness and uncertainty, shifted slightly, and her racing pulse began to calm.

'I wonder if today's children use it for the same purpose?' Her tone was a pale imitation of his matter-of-factness.

'I doubt it. They're much more sophisticated in many ways.' He shifted slightly to half-turn towards her, resting an arm along the back of the seat. 'You don't look as though you've slept much. I'd forgotten how hopeless you are after rows. As a youth it always seemed incredible to me that you could flare up at the drop of a hat and yet go about white-faced and pinched-looking for hours after. I see you haven't changed.'

Nicola shrugged and at last turned to look at him full-faced. 'You have the unhappy knack of making me feel a child again,' she said.

'Ah ... that is a pity,' Michael replied, considering her. The joggers came by at a brisk trot and gave a cheery greeting. 'About last night,' Michael went on, 'I offended you, implying Cassandra wasn't safe in your care. I'm sorry. I plead concern for you both that made me put it to you so clumsily. Will you forgive me?' He waited and added drily, 'If the words stick, you could always nod your head.'

Relief was like the onrush of a spring bursting from the ground. They could be friends again! 'I do understand how you must worry over Cass, and I'm sorry I hit you.'

'I didn't hear that too well,' Michael said, sliding along the seat. 'What did you say, Red?' He lifted her mitten-covered hand and tucked it companionably through his arm, his body solid against her.

She eyed him warily. 'I said I'm sorry I hit you.'

'That's what I thought you said, but I wanted to have it confirmed. Two apologies are always better than one.'

Nicola burst out laughing. 'How underhand you are, Michael,' she reproached. 'I shall rescind one, if not both!'

'You can't. It isn't allowed. Once evidence is given . . .' His eyes rested thoughtfully on her face. 'I'm sorry about the kiss. It was . . . rather a drastic way of proving my point, and not at all satisfactory. Things done in anger rarely are.' He pulled off a glove and touched her cheek, his fingers warm against her skin, and gently brushed his lips against hers.

Nicola's lashes fluttered and a delicate pink tinged her cheeks and she became stupidly tongue-tied! Michael grinned wickedly.

'I seem to recall kissing you once before when I was—oh, about fourteen, I think, during a family party. For a dare, if my memory serves me right. You slapped my face that time too, I should have remembered last night, and ducked.'

A bubble of laughter exploded in Nicola's throat. The tension had lightened.

'I suppose I should be grateful you didn't kick me on the shins, another delightful habit of yours,' Michael went on drily. 'Victor tells me you haven't eaten breakfast. There's a parcel to be collected from the post office so I suggest we remove ourselves from this extremely uncomfortable seat before we freeze to death. The car's parked at the bottom of the hill. We'll stop off at Moffat's and then call for the parcel on the way back.' Michael stood up, bringing her with him, and they set off at a trot down the hill.

Nicola was glad of his arm for support. She had tossed and turned during the night, bemoaning her wretched temper, berating first herself and then Michael for the things they both had said. Now everything was all right again.

Moffat's was in the High Street, a home-made bread, cakes and pastry shop with a rear room taken over for morning snacks and afternoon teas. Inside it was warm and cosy and the smell from the bakery was tantalisingly appetising. There were a few shoppers taking the weight from their feet as Michael and Nicola entered and selected a window table. Tea and buttered toast was brought on request and a companionable silence ensued while they got on with the business of eating.

At least, Nicola ate, Michael merely watched approvingly as he drank his tea. Nicola poured out a second cup for herself and said:

'It was good of you to let Cassandra keep Hamlet.' She flicked him a glance. 'I presume you asked Victor's permission?'

Michael smiled but he did not deny it. Some devil prompted Nicola to continue:

'Victor thinks you could do with a wife.' She took a sip from the cup, wondering how far she should go. 'I'm inclined to agree with him.'

'How thoughtful of you both. You must get together with Aunt Margaret, she'll be delighted to have you on her side.'

'It would solve a few problems, wouldn't it?'

'But not the best of reasons. If, and when, I decide to take a wife, you will all be informed. Until then, I shall be grateful if you would keep your twitching noses to yourselves!'

Nicola grinned and reached for another piece of toast. Michael's glance landed on her wrist.

'Did I do that?' he exclaimed as he took her hand and frowned down at the marks of battle. 'What a brute I am.'

'I bruise very easily—I always have,' Nicola said quickly, jumping slightly as a voice above them said sharply:

'Michael! Nicola! I didn't think to find you here.'

Without haste, Michael released Nicola's hand and slowly rose to his feet. 'Aunt Margaret, this is a surprise,' he declared pleasantly. 'Would you care to join us? As you see, we have nearly finished, but I can soon ask for more, if you wish?'

Margaret Dalmain was a well-preserved woman whose looks were slightly marred by the hint of dissatisfaction in the set of her mouth. Her hair, once fair like her son Kit's, was now white and groomed in regimental waves, and her figure was regal. She was looking at her nephew with censure and Nicola with suspicion and thinly veiled dislike.

Nicola had known about the dislike, even as a child, and had learned to keep out of Margaret Dalmain's way as much as possible, perfecting an innocent, wide-eyed look with which to parry accusations, advice or whatever else her aunt-by-permission delivered.

Margaret now refused the offer of tea, her eyes sweeping the table and returning to land on her nephew with an expression demanding some explanation. Michael, not easily intimidated, disappointed her by not offering one, and squiring her back to her own table where he was introduced to a waiting friend, charmed this friend and soothed his aunt's ruffled feathers with a few choice words.

When he returned Nicola had finished off the

toast and had drunk her tea. Standing by her chair, leaning forward, one hand on the table, the other on the chair-back, Michael murmured:

'Shall we go? I'll settle up while you make your farewell to Auntie,' and he gave her a wicked smile. Nicola, aware of Aunt Margaret's eagle eye still upon them, refrained from returning it and reluctantly made her way over. She was introduced to the friend as 'poor Joan's niece.' Nicola wanted to laugh but controlled herself. She could imagine her Auntie Joan giving a conspiratorial wink, agreeing that the 'poor' was ambiguous. Did it refer to Joan's untimely death, or the fact that Nicola was her niece?

Nicola was then put through a barrage of questions and answered them with as much polite brevity as she could muster. How was Adele and her husband? Did Adele like living in America? How long would Nicola be at Bredon House? After the questions came the statements ... that Cassandra was running wild and Noel was getting insolent, he had actually disagreed with her the other day, became quite defiant. It was time Michael married that charming Geraldine Forest— her father was such a splendid man, and could influence Michael's career, a matter not to be viewed lightly.

Margaret did not, however, ask Nicola why she and Michael were at Moffat's, for which Nicola was grateful, for she couldn't think of a single explanation that would have sounded feasible.

When Nicola finally joined Michael, he asked, eyes dancing: 'Have you emerged unscathed?' while raising an arm in farewell to his aunt, who was looking pointedly in their direction, before ushering Nicola out into the High Street.

'Just,' admitted Nicola, and wondered if Aunt Margaret was right about Geraldine Forest—she had a habit of knowing everyone's business first.

Quickening his stride, Michael said: 'You can pick up your parcel while I get back to the car. We're dangerously near the parking limit.'

'*My* parcel?' queried Nicola in surprise. At the post office she was handed a brown paper packet, re-directed in Jennie's hand-writing. *Code Name Fox* actually in her possession at last!

In the safety of her room she unwrapped the brown paper and her own personal copies lay before her. The cover was red, bright and noticeable, with black Japanese lettering diagonally across the front forming the shape of a dagger. Nicola smoothed her hand over it, grinning idiotically. She opened the cover and began to turn the pages.

The feeling was incredible, almost as if someone else had written it!

She bundled the copies back into the packet and hid them in the bottom of the wardrobe.

December arrived with the weather worsening and snow falling. After a week of exceptionally hard frosts, Ulverscroft Pool froze over and skates were brought out of storage and the ice tested for safety. Noel and Cassandra were well aware of the dangers of iced ponds, having heard how Kit and Michael had very nearly lost their lives when the ice cracked and gave way one year.

'Were you with them, Nickie?' Noel asked when this story was again brought out and aired on the way to the pool, and Nicola shook her head.

'It happened the winter before I came,' she said, giving Noel an amused look. 'I wasn't responsible for every escapade that happened in the past, Noel!'

Her cousin grinned, saying innocently, 'Oh, were you not?' and Kit, sitting in front, with Michael driving the Ford, crowed with amusement and leaned back and snatched off Nicola's woolly hat, chortling.

'See what a reputation you have, Nick!'

It was an afternoon of pure nostalgia. Nicola felt sixteen again and when Kit grabbed her, yelling, 'Let's do a Torvill and Dean' which turned out to be more a Laurel and Hardy, she felt her sides would burst with the strain of laughing.

Fox on the Rocks began to take off, and when Michael went to Amsterdam on business she had three days to have a good go at it.

Noel was in a play performed by the sixth form college and Nicola and Cassandra went to see him in it. Noel had one of the leading roles and afterwards Nicola found herself talking to the drama tutor and was able to say, with sincerity, how good she thought the play had been, and Noel in particular had surprised her.

The tutor replied, 'Thank you, I'm glad you enjoyed it. They all worked hard and did very well, especially Noel. He has talent, your cousin. Wants to take it up professionally, I understand?'

'Take it up?' echoed Nicola. 'Acting, do you mean?'

'Yes. So he was saying the other week.' The tutor's expression changed. 'Have I let the cat out of the bag?'

Nicola smiled. 'I think you have. It's the first I've heard of Noel wanting to act.'

'The family is in publishing, isn't it?' the tutor asked.

'One branch is, and it's expected that Noel will join the family firm,' explained Nicola thoughtfully. 'Noel's elder brother is a barrister.'

'It might be a passing phase,' the tutor offered, 'though knowing young Noel, I doubt it. Here he is now. I'd better apologise for speaking out of turn.' He greeted Noel, congratulating him on his performance, going on to say: 'I'm afraid I've mentioned your interest in the professional stage, Noel. Sorry.'

Noel shot Nicola a quick look before saying: 'That's okay, sir. I don't mind my cousin knowing.'

The tutor smiled, relieved. 'Good. No harm done, then. Now, if you'll excuse me, I think I'm wanted,' and nodding in a friendly manner, he moved off.

Noel stared a little defiantly at Nicola. 'Now you know.'

'Is this why you've been like a bear with a sore head for the past weeks, Noel?'

He grinned sheepishly. 'I don't want to disappoint Michael.'

'Well, he certainly won't want you to go for a career that your heart isn't set on. And he knows what it's all about, doesn't he? He opted out, didn't he? It's a pity he couldn't have seen you tonight, it might have done some good. You really were excellent, Noel.'

'Thanks.' Noel's face pinked with pleasure. He gave a shrug. 'As for Michael, I'm auditioning in January for drama school and if I get accepted then I'll tell him, there's no point if I'm turned down. You won't say anything to him, will you, Nickie?'

'Only if you promise to buck your ideas up

where Michael's concerned. It's not his fault you're feeling mixed up and guilty and he can't help you if you don't tell him, can he?'

Noel grinned, 'I'm glad you know, Nickie.'

The following evening Cassandra lifted her head from her books and said, 'Michael's home tomorrow, isn't he?'

'Mmm . . . should be,' answered Nicola, licking a finger where she had jabbed it with the needle, sewing on a button to one of her blouses. Something in Cassandra's voice made her ask, 'Do you miss him, Cass?'

Cassandra nodded. 'I hate it when he's away, but I don't tell him, of course, what good would it do?' She smiled shyly at her cousin. 'It's so nice having you here, Nickie, but it can't last, can it?' and Cassandra's head went down again into her books.

How vulnerable one was at fourteen, thought Nicola. It was such an in-between age, neither child nor adult, on the threshold of womanhood. A time of fluctuating between bouts of insecurity and fighting for independence. Had she done more harm than good filling in here at Bredon House? When she left would the contrast be even more severe?

She said casually, 'The first free day we get we'll go into Town and get you a new dress for Aunt and Uncle's Ruby party, eh?' and Cassandra nodded happily.

Jennie put forward her matchmaking plans by inviting Nicola to join Bill and herself, and a colleague of Bill's, to her birthday treat—a programme of contemporary dance at Sadler's Wells. Nicola enjoyed herself, and given a bit of encouragement, Bill's friend would have pressed for another meeting, but she couldn't stir up enough energy to be bothered. He was a nice enough fellow, but . . .

Nicola had left the Beetle at Ashwell Station. Driving home she remembered that Michael was due back today and found herself agreeing with Cassandra—he might be infuriating at times, but his presence was oddly reassuring.

She discovered him sitting sprawled in an armchair before the fire, reading, Hamlet across one foot. She made a pot of tea and they watched a documentary on Japan that Nicola was glad she hadn't missed and then brought him up to date with the family news, such as she was able.

Reaching out for Michael's cup to give him a refill she accidentally knocked the book he had been reading from off the arm of the chair and picked it up, her apology broken off mid-way as she stared at the cover. Unnoticed before, as Michael had placed it cover down, she felt herself going red.

Mistaking surprise for curiosity, Michael said, 'That's one of our new ones. Kit passed it on for me to read, a first attempt, so I understand.'

Nicola handed him back the book and busied herself with the tea-pot. She asked casually, 'Are you enjoying it?' and waited, in an agony of anticipation, almost dreading the answer.

'I'm only half-way through,' Michael replied, pausing to give the question his full consideration. 'It's certainly not the usual run-of-the-mill spy story. The characters have some depth, and it has a good, racy style.' He took the offered cup. 'Yes . . . I am enjoying it.'

A feeling of exquisite pleasure swept over

Nicola. 'I didn't think you went in for those kind of books, Michael.'

He eyed her teasing face with equanimity. 'Sometimes it's the only kind of book to read when you've had a brute of a day,' he answered. 'My taste is varied. I only ask that a book is well written, and this is. You can borrow it after me, if you wish.'

'Thank you, I'd like to,' was all she could say.

'Kit calls him their mystery man.' Michael observed the glossy cover. 'N. A. Merchant refuses to go to the office and keeps contact by letter. Kit thinks its probably some prissy civil servant who wants to remain anonymous for fear of shocking the establishment! Be that as it may, Kit believes that our mystery man has found the happy knack of writing a spy story that is readable for both men and women.'

No more questions, Nicola warned herself, enough is enough, and drank her tea, feeling as though she had drunk a bottle of champagne. Michael liked her writing! Her eyes rested pensively upon Michael's hands, still holding the book. He had beautiful hands . . .

'Red?'

She came to with a jump, saying with a laugh: 'Sorry, I was dreaming . . .'

'I asked if you'd seen anything of Aunt and Uncle, or Kit, this week?'

'I had lunch with Kit on Wednesday, a hurried affair, he had to rush off for an appointment.' She put her empty cup on the nearby low table. 'Any reason for asking? I think they're all well.'

'Mmm . . .? No, no . . . Kit picked me up from the airport and we had a drink together. He was about to meet his parents for a meal, they were all joining the Keynes, so he told me.' His eyes rested on her gravely.

'They seem to be seeing a lot of the Keynes lately. Sooner them than me,' joked Nicola, rising to her feet and allowing a yawn to escape her. Hamlet jumped up, tail wagging.

'I'll take the dog out,' offered Michael and Nicola bent to scratch the shaggy curls on the top of Hamlet's head.

'Will you? Thanks. He'll have to go on the lead, I'm afraid. He doesn't know the meaning of the word obedience yet.'

Michael glanced at the dog who had now rolled on to his back, legs waving in the air as Nicola transferred the scratching to his belly.

'I've already found that out,' he informed her. 'The wretched animal seems to have taken a liking to my slippers. We had quite a tussle over ownership.'

Nicola chuckled. 'He's intelligent. What he's trying to do is bring them to you.'

'Really? You do surprise me,' Michael said drily, 'and whoever's trying to teach him to bring in the newspaper, would you ask them to stop? I find no pleasure in a chewed-up, soggy mass of newsprint.'

Nicola laughed outright. 'What a spoil-sport you are, Michael.'

'You wait until he takes something of yours,' warned Michael, his eyes following her to the door. 'Red . . .'

She stopped and turned an enquiring face.

Michael regarded her, eyes hooded, and then gave a slight shake of the head. 'No matter . . . good night,' he said at last, his eyes remaining fixed on her for a few seconds before he returned to his reading.

'Good night, Michael.' Nicola took a last look at the dark head bent over the book, the flickering fire, Hamlet's buttonbright eyes peering round the chair, photographing the scene in her mind's eye to be recalled later.

CHAPTER FIVE

THE boiler at Cassandra's school packed up and the building was closed for three days.

'Good. We'll go to Town to get your dress,' Nicola told her cousin and on hearing of the outing, Michael offered to give them a lift in.

During the journey, taken in the Ford, the Jaguar accommodating only two comfortably, Cassandra said:

'Are you in court today, Michael?' and when her brother admitted that he was, she went on, 'Could we come? I haven't been for ages and it won't take all day to buy a dress, will it, Nickie? Would you like to see Michael in court?'

'Mmm . . . yes, I would.' Nicola glanced at him, face dead-pan. 'I've always wondered what he looks like in his wig and gown.'

'He looks very distinguished,' Cassandra declared proudly.

Michael drawled: 'I'm flattered, but can't guarantee a particularly dramatic session. It's a fraud case. You might even find it boring.'

'Won't you be speaking?' asked Cassandra, disappointed.

'I shall do my fair share,' Michael replied.

'That's all we're going for, isn't it, Nickie?' Cassandra said cheerfully.

Nicola grinned, 'With justice running a close second.'

Michael murmured, 'Justice as well, eh? I'll have to see what can be done.'

Boring, or not, the court was quite full and the case much more important than Michael had led them to believe. As he entered, he glanced up and smiled slightly and Cassandra turned to Nicola. 'All my friends are madly in love with Michael— they think he's gorgeous,' she whispered.

The array of wigs and robes, and the entrance of the judge in scarlet gave a theatrical element to the proceedings, thought Nicola, her eyes straying back to Michael.

He had told them on the way in that his case rested on proving that his client was the innocent victim, unknowingly aiding his partners in the fraud. Even though the ins-and-outs of stocks and shares and company business was way above their heads, the two cousins waited with baited breath as Michael rose to his feet to cross-examine the other two men involved. Watched them lulled by his soothing, confidential manner to eventually fall into the trap Michael had set for them. As he swung away, satisfied, he glanced up and his left eye-lid quivered in an audacious wink before he bent his head to speak to a colleague.

When court was adjourned for lunch they met up, as planned, the foyer of the court building teaming with people. As Michael came striding towards them, papers beneath his arm, he said regretfully:

'I'm sorry, I was hoping to eat with you, but something's cropped up which has to be looked into before court sits again.' His eyes moved beyond them and he nodded and called: 'I won't be a moment,' and both Cassandra and Nicola automatically turned round and saw Geraldine Forest, wigged and gowned, holding a file, who smiled as she waited for Michael to join her.

'We quite understand,' Nicola said briskly, and making arrangements to meet up later at Michael's Chambers, they left.

When Cassandra and Noel came down the stairs on the evening of the 'Ruby' party Nicola looked them over and decided with cousinly pride that they would do. Noel was in evening suit, for the party was a formal affair, and looked very adult. Nicola felt a stab of shock as he came towards her, for it was difficult to believe that this good-looking young man was the red squalling baby she had held, only a few hours after his birth! Where had all the years gone? What had she done with them?

A swish of material caught her eye as Cassandra minced her way down the stairs, following her brother, trying to look sophisticated until it proved too much and she broke into giggles halfway down. The dress, that she and Nicola had jealously guarded until this moment, was shot silk taffeta in a deep aquamarine colour with a boat-shaped neck, three-quarter sleeves and a very full skirt, nipped in at the waist with a wide belt. Nicola thought she looked lovely and her approving glance lingered on the silver-grey pumps and small evening bag, rising to the newly washed hair that had been trimmed to frame her face.

'Well?' Cassandra demanded of Michael, who unbeknown to Nicola had walked quietly from the study into the hall and was standing outside her line of vision. 'Will we do?'

'Indeed you will, both of you,' responded Michael warmly, adding teasingly, 'It gives me renewed hope that one day you will actually reach adulthood and be off my hands.'

'I shall be, in the New Year,' announced Noel

challengingly. 'An adult, I mean,' and then threw an apologetic glance at Nicola.

'So you shall,' soothed Michael.

Cassandra broke in impatiently, 'I think twenty-one is much more sensible, and you haven't said anything about Nicola, Michael! Don't you think she looks fantastic? It's from New York. Fifth Avenue!'

Nicola froze, feeling suddenly exposed. She shot Michael a quick glance and found herself enveloped by his lazy, over-long appraisal.

'Aunt Margaret will love it,' Michael murmured, running the tip of his finger down her bare spine. 'Very elegant and quite outrageous.'

'Thank you,' said Nicola, 'and it wasn't Aunt Margaret I had in mind when I bought it.'

Michael grinned. 'No. I thought not.' He walked round her, brows raised. 'Did it break the bank, Red?'

'Mother and Neil bought it for me,' she replied, feeling ridiculously like a girl out to her first ball and not liking the feeling. The dress was black and simple and suited her tall, slim figure, but it was eye-catching, and tonight she had chosen it with a view to annoying Aunt Margaret, and Michael knew it.

'Well, I think I'd better book the supper dance right now,' Michael said, holding out the white fake fur coat so that she could slip her hands down the sleeves. The cool silk lining touched her skin and she felt a shiver ripple through her and she seemed incredibly aware of Michael, standing behind her, his hands resting on her shoulders as he settled the coat round her. The whole thing could hardly have taken a few seconds, but it seemed as if the action had been slowed, and

Cassandra and Noel were frozen into a tableau and only she and Michael were living and breathing.

The illusion was broken by Cassandra, 'It's a dream of a dress, Nickie,' and turning to her elder brother she added tragically, 'Oh, Michael, it's lovely having Nickie here with us. How foul it will be when she has to leave!'

'I quite agree, Cass, my love,' replied Michael, leaving Nicola and helping Cassandra on with her coat, 'but we can't expect Nicola to stay too long. You know what a restless soul she is.'

But I've changed! For a moment Nicola thought she had said the words out loud, but they were only in her head. Michael turned to look at her, smiling teasingly. She felt distanced from her body, seeing the woman in the black dress and the white fur coat and the man in evening suit as strangers, acutely aware of each other as strangers are at first meeting, when perception is sharpened by curiosity.

'I don't think we shall let Aunt Margaret down,' Michael observed whimsically, his eyes passing over them, one by one.

Noel grinned. 'Poor Auntie is never too sure of us, is she?'

'With good reason, sometimes,' declared Michael drily. 'This is an important night for her, so we'll all be on our best behaviour, mmm . . .?'

'Forty years married!' intoned Cassandra in awe. 'Poor Uncle Rupert!' and then, seeing her elder brother's face, clapped her hand over her mouth contritely. 'Sorry.'

Face dead-pan, Michael ordered: 'Out, young woman,' but as his sister and brother passed in front he shot Nicola a comical look as she went before him and she shook her head in sympathy.

The Ford was parked in readiness, the path to it cleared of snow, and Michael asked: 'Like to drive, Noel?' and tossed the keys to his brother who caught them and managed a nonchalant: 'Okay.'

Nicola sat in the back with Cassandra, listening with half an ear to the conversation going on around her. She felt most peculiar, keyed-up and taut, as if tonight was important. She gave a wry smile in the semi-darkness and realised she had caught some of Cassandra's excitement of dressing up for a special occasion, although she had ambivalent feelings about the 'Ruby' party itself. Rupert and Kit had never considered her anything but a true member of the Dalmain family, but Margaret had always made her aware of her only tenuous connections.

Nicola's eyes rested thoughtfully on Michael, sitting in front. He was talking to Noel, voice relaxed, and yet she knew that part of his attention was on the road ahead and on Noel driving. There was a thoroughness about Michael that was strangely comforting these days. There was a time when his quietly confident, self-contained manner was an instant challenge, but somehow, it didn't seem to bother her any more.

Michael glanced over his shoulder. 'Everything all right, Red?' he asked. 'You're very quiet.' She made an appropriate reply and then the lights from the hotel could be seen through the trees and Noel drove into the carpark.

Margaret and Rupert Dalmain were welcoming their guests at the entrance to the large ballroom they had taken over for their anniversary party. As coats were taken from them Rupert stepped forward, face beaming with pleasure and his eyes encompassed them all. He bent to kiss the girls.

'Nicola, Cassandra, my dears, how delightful you both look.' Rupert was a tall man with grey, receding hair and kindly brown eyes set in a thin, cavernous face. He shook hands with his nephews. 'Noel, Michael, glad you could make it.' He turned his head and called, 'Margaret! Here is the family.'

Margaret had been talking to another guest and now joined her husband. She allowed each of them a peck at her cheek and thanked Michael for their combined gift of crystal glass-ware, her eyes drifting over them, coming to rest on Nicola.

She had never taken to the girl, even from the beginning. Possibly because she sensed an intractability, a stubbornness in Nicola's make-up that she had neither the right nor the power to subdue. She considered this step-niece a bad influence upon Kit in their youth and for one period had been dismayed at the prospect that Nicola might well become her daughter-in-law. Thankfully, Kit had come to his senses and nothing had come of it, although the threat had always been there, a possibility that Kit might succumb to the girl's charisma, which existed, so she was told, although she herself could never see evidence of it. However, the threat was no longer viable and with this thought in mind Margaret could afford to relax.

'Auntie's overdone the glitter a bit, don't you think?' whispered Cassandra, as they moved into the ballroom. 'She'd be a good decoration for the Christmas Tree!'

'Hush, behave yourself,' ordered Nicola, controlling the impulse to smile.

'This cannot be ... yes, yes, it is! Miss Cassandra Dalmain in person!' With his voice full of wonder and admiration Kit whirled his young cousin round. 'Very nice ... very nice,' he exclaimed seriously and Cassandra went pink with pleasure. 'I'll have the first dance with you, Cass, my lovely, or else I'll not get a look in.' His eyes passed on to Nicola and he gave a soft whistle. 'You look stunning, Miss Redford.'

She graciously inclined her head, replying demurely, 'Thank you, Mr Dalmain, you look rather dishy yourself,' and they stood smiling at each other.

Cassandra excused herself and darted off to join a friend. Kit, serious for a moment, said, 'I want to talk to you, Nick. Hopeless for a bit. Save me the dance after the food, will you?' and before Nicola could do more than give her agreement, Hester Keynes drifted up, dressed in floating blue chiffon and looking extremely beautiful, and tucked her arm through Kit's. She smiled.

'Hello, Nicola—lovely to see you ... Kit, do come! I want you to meet...'

Kit was led away, throwing a laughing apology over his shoulder. A hand closed Nicola's fingers round the stem of a glass, transferring then to her arm as she was steered further into the room, stopping at a table on the edge of the dance floor.

'Drink up,' he ordered, raising his own glass to his lips as Michael's eyes travelled round the room. 'I think we'll need fortifying. I've just spied Great Aunt Maud, and my goodness that surely can't be Uncle Wallace!' He ignored Nicola's giggle and continued to view the proceedings with cool detachment, the hint of amusement echoed in eyes and mouth. 'Quite a social gathering,' he went on.

'Prestige and wealth mingling with relations we only meet at funerals and weddings.'

At the far end of the ballroom a small orchestra began to play a popular song and Noel came up and asked Nicola to dance.

'I'll limber up with you first, Nickie, as practise,' he said with a cheeky grin, 'while I cast my eyes over the possibilities.'

'I'm honoured,' replied Nicola, stepping on to the floor, unaware of the interest she was causing in a number of male guests. 'But let's not get too energetic, eh? I don't want to disgrace myself forever in the eyes of Aunt Margaret and shake myself right out of this dress!'

The dances were a mixture of old and new, in deference to the wide range of ages present. Noel and Cassandra quickly met up with other young guests and relatives and appeared to be having a good time. Nicola knew many people there and wandered round, talking, catching up on news, being constantly whisked on to the dance floor. She was aware of Kit everywhere, being supportive in his rôle as son of the house, dragging shy guests on to the floor and dancing with his usual eye-catching energy, talking seriously with business associates or leading more matronly guests into the veleta and military-twostep with great panache. As he passed Nicola during one of these old-time medleys he hissed, 'The dance after supper!' and then he was gone and Nicola returned her attention back to a rather chinless wonder who droned on about his golf handicap. When the dance finished and he removed his hot sticky hands Nicola felt like telling him he had more than one handicap.

She caught sight of Michael sauntering leisurely

round the room, lingering to talk, his eyes taking everything in. He took to the dance floor occasionally and let himself go in a rather hectic modern jive with Cassandra, among all the young people, which raised a few cheers.

Hester coaxed both Kit and Michael on to the floor and seemed never to be without a partner. She was in a vivacious, bubbling mood and everything about her sparkled. To Nicola's surprise Chapman Keynes cornered her and subjected her to a keen cross-examination of her life and prospects with a bluntness she found difficult to parry. She was glad when Michael wandered up and joined them and talk became more general. She was amused to watch the skill with which Michael handled the older man, but then, handling people and words was Michael's daily bread.

Supper was announced and Cassandra and Noel returned to the family table, and food was consumed amidst much hilarity and family joking. Chapman Keynes gave a toast from the top table to Margaret and Rupert, to which Rupert replied, his speech short, but witty.

'It must cost Margaret dear to stay silent,' Michael murmured for Nicola's ear only and she spluttered her drink and glared at him reproachfully.

Supper over, the orchestra returned and swept into a waltz. Remembering Kit's orders to keep the dance after the food for him, Nicola looked round, searching for him, and after a moment caught sight of his fair head close to a dark one, Hester's. Nicola gave a mental shrug and drained her glass, refilling it from the bottle on the table. Before she could raise it to her lips Michael took it from her, saying firmly:

'I don't think we can let the evening go by without dancing together, do you, Red? This tempo is more suited to my advancing years,' and he rose to his feet, looking down at her, eyes mocking as he added: 'I seem to remember suffering bruised toes at the time you were learning to trip the light fantastic.'

'Then it's brave of you to ask me now,' retorted Nicola, her eyes belying the challenge in her voice.

'Well—I've been observing you closely during the evening,' Michael returned suavely, 'and find you much improved.'

She burst out laughing. 'Beast! For that I ought to refuse you!'

'But you won't.'

The laughter stuck in her throat and she caught her breath, feeling winded. She heard the gentle coaxing of his voice and saw the wicked glint of laughter in his eyes and the world turned over, once again.

No—of course she wouldn't refuse him! For hadn't she been waiting and waiting and hoping for him to ask her all evening? Unaware of the music and the jostling of other couples taking to the floor Nicola stood and stared at this man she had known for almost all her life. Stared, and was hit by an incredible self-awareness, so amazing and so ridiculously obvious, that she stood speechless, struggling inside, trying to cope and accept the truth about herself.

'But you won't, will you?' The question lingered unanswered and Michael drew her, unresisting, on to the dance floor. 'Just think what a blow it would be to my self-esteem if you did!'

The electrifying fusion as his hand took hers sent Nicola into blind panic. She allowed herself to be drawn close, because she was helpless to stop it, and flinched as his hand went round her waist and rested cool and firm on the bare flesh of her back.

They began to dance. Her limbs moved of their own accord, she had no mind or will to control them and needed none—Michael was in control, his body moved and swirled, taking her with him. All Nicola could think about was how to get through the rest of the evening without making a fool of herself.

Michael! Surely she couldn't be that much of an imbecile? After all these years, surely it can't be Michael? She closed her eyes, fighting for a clear head—oh, why had she drunk that last glass of wine!

She breathed in the heady male smell of him, feeling the texture of his suit beneath her hand, his breath warm on her cheek, his body fitting so extraordinarily right with hers.

Their steps shortened as the numbers increased on the floor. Was she imagining this amazing feeling of belonging? She moved her head cautiously, glancing at his face. Michael caught the movement and smiled slightly, eyes curiously expressionless, lids lowered, but he did not break the silence between them. She returned the smile, but her face was stiff and she doubted it was one of her best. She lowered her own lids, her eyes lingering on his mouth, and thought how easy it would be to press her lips against his . . .

She wrenched her eyes away and gave a silent groan, clenching her teeth together. How could it be *Michael*, of *all* people? Michael, whom she had disliked for years? . . . and she fought down a bubble of laughter that threatened to explode from her lips. What a poor fool she was! What a blind, idiotic fool!

Afterwards it was difficult to put what happened next into the right order, for it obviously was beginning before she was aware of it. The music faded and drew to a close and as their steps ceased Michael released her and Nicola breathed a sigh of relief—her bones ached with the effort of trying to be relaxed and she longed to look at him properly, and daren't. Scattered applause sounded and gathering together all her reserves of self-preservation Nicola said in a bright voice: 'Thank you, Michael,' and allowed herself a casual glance, catching a sharp, interrogating look in response— what on earth did she look like to make him look at her like that, she wondered, and directed her gaze desperately elsewhere. What had been going on before the dance had even finished was now heralded by a cheer and on one section of the dance floor the dancers parted to disclose Hester and Kit being urged towards the platform.

Nicola heard Michael give a muttered exclamation and he began to push his way through the dancers, now all looking towards the disturbance, taking Nicola with him. Looking back over her shoulder Nicola could see that Kit, realising that they had attracted the attention of the whole ballroom, was raising his hands for silence.

She stopped, resisting Michael's lead, and he waited beside her. And still she did not understand. Why should she? A much more important occurrence had just happened to her and she could hardly take anything else in with coherence.

Stepping up on to the stage, helping Hester to follow, Kit said something to the leader of the orchestra who smiled, and gestured to the microphone.

'Ladies and gentlemen,' Kit began, 'friends, relatives—I think you've guessed what I am about to say . . .'

There was a burst of laughter and Kit smiled down at Hester. Nicola was thinking: now I really shall have to leave Bredon House. I can't go on living there, seeing Michael every day, trying to act normal. Nothing will ever be normal again . . .

'We were not going to make our announcement this evening,' Kit was saying, 'as we felt that it was Mother and Father's day, but they have given us their blessing, and surrounded by all of you who wish us well, we couldn't hold out any longer.'

More laughter and cheers. Michael took Nicola firmly by the arm and walked her the few paces to their table, almost forcing her into her chair. She obeyed the pressure of his hand, looking at him blankly.

'As you've guessed,' Kit continued, 'Hester has done me the honour of promising to become my wife.' He turned to the radiant woman at his side and raised her hand to his lips and amidst further clapping and cheers and calls of congratulations, Chapman Keynes stepped up, a broad, powerful figure, joined by Kit's parents—Rupert smiling benignly, Margaret triumphantly.

Chapman kissed his daughter and shook Kit by the hand before turning to the waiting guests.

He said: 'I was honoured to make a toast earlier, to Margaret and Rupert, and now it gives me the greatest of pleasure to make another—to my daughter, Hester, and to Christopher, their son . . . an alliance between our two families we are delighted to witness. I am sure you will join with us in wishing Hester and Christopher every happiness in their future together. Ladies and gentlemen—Hester and Christopher.'

Michael put a glass into Nicola's hand and she obediently drank the toast.

CHAPTER SIX

'WELL! Hester and Kit! Who'd have thought it!' exclaimed Cassandra, as they were going home. 'Did *you* know what was going on, Michael?'

Her brother said: 'I had some idea—nothing official.' His eyes went to the mirror and Nicola, meeting them, looked away.

'Bit quick, isn't it?' Noel stated.

In an amused voice Michael answered, 'Some people decide in minutes.'

'Why didn't you tell us?' queried Cassandra, slightly aggrieved.

'My dear child—what was there to tell? Only that Kit seemed to be seeing Hester rather a lot over the past few weeks and that your aunt and uncle have entertained the Keynes more frequently than warranted a merely casual acquaintance.'

'Why Christopher?' demanded Cassandra indignantly. 'He's always been Kit. Is she going to make everyone call him Christopher, do you think?'

'I have no idea,' responded Michael calmly, 'but I doubt it. Tonight tended towards formality, didn't it? In any event, he'll always be Kit to us.'

'Of course he will.' Noel gave a yawn. 'It wasn't a bad party, considering.'

'The food was good,' agreed Cassandra, catching his yawn and leaning her head comfortably on Nicola's shoulder. 'Did you enjoy it, Nickie?' she went on sleepily, and Nicola murmured:

'Yes. Don't fall asleep Cass. You'll feel awful if you do and we're nearly home.'

Home . . . but not for much longer, she thought wistfully. Her eyes returned to Michael, sitting behind the wheel, silent now and frowning at the road ahead. He had been kindly protective for the rest of the evening, hardly leaving her side, and it was not until Great Aunt Maud had said: 'Let Kit slip through your fingers, eh, silly girl? You can't keep 'em waiting about forever, you know!' that Nicola had realised why. She didn't care what Maud or anyone else thought, but Michael was different. She minded dreadfully Michael having the wrong impression about her and Kit.

Fate hadn't been very kind, dealing her two blows within minutes of each other. It was bad enough realising she was hopelessly involved with Michael—hopeless, helpless and hooked—without depriving her of her only ally, Kit. For nothing would be the same again, with Kit, and among all the anguish of Michael was a tiny bit of hurt that Kit hadn't confided in her . . . but even that was probably unreasonable. She couldn't tell him about Michael to save her life! Well, perhaps that was going too far but it made the point.

When they could get near the happy couple Michael had gone with her to congratulate them. By this time Nicola had consumed two more glasses of wine and was finding herself extremely witty, and after Maud's revealing comment, it was necessary to appear lighthearted and unconcerned. Kit had accepted her congratulatory kiss on the cheek with a laughing, slightly sheepish air, Hester with smooth, silky sweetness. As for Aunt Margaret, she was nearly bursting with pride and achievement and had so far forgotten herself as to kiss Nicola with warmth on saying goodbye! Remembering this now, Nicola felt a stab of compunction—poor Aunt Margaret, did she realise what she was up against? Hester, sweet and pliable now, will bide her time.

'Wake up, Nickie!' chuckled Cassandra, and Nicola opened her eyes as the headlights caught the house in a moving arch.

'I wasn't asleep,' Nicola told her. Michael pulled up at the front door to allow them to alight and then drove on to put the car away.

'Oh, lor' I'm tired,' yawned Cassandra, staggering up the stairs. She turned at the bend and leaned over the bannister. 'Thank you for choosing me such a lovely dress, Nickie ... everyone said how nice it was. Goodnight,' and she yawned loudly again and plodded on.

'Victor's left a note—he's taken Hamlet out,' said Noel, following her up. ''Night,' and Nicola, now joined by Michael, said goodnight in return.

'Do you want a drink, Red?' Michael asked, entering the sitting room and discarding his coat and tie. He walked to the drinks' cabinet and began to pour himself a brandy. Nicola said: 'No, thanks,' and crossed to the fire which still had the glowing embers of a log burning. She sank to her knees on the hearth rug and slipped off her shoes, wiggling her toes with a degree of thankfulness. She watched Michael cross to the tape rack, select one and slide it into the deck. As the opening bars of the classical guitar music began she quickly looked away, not wanting to be caught watching him. She took the combs out of her hair, dropping them one by one into her lap and ran fingers through the freed strands, shaking her head and enjoying the feeling of release it gave.

Suddenly aware of Michael's stillness, she lifted her head and found he was watching her, his face, for that fraction of a second as her eyes met his, oddly austere.

She said quietly: 'Michael, why didn't you tell me about Hester and Kit?'

Michael took a drink from his glass and settled himself in a chair, tossing out a cushion so that he had more room. 'I thought I explained in the car,' he said.

Nicola swept the combs into the palm of her hand and dropped them into her evening bag, shutting the clasp with frowning concentration. Her hair fell forward and she pushed it back impatiently, her eyes regarding him steadily as she said evenly:

'You explained why you hadn't mentioned it to Noel and Cass. I was different, surely?'

There was silence. Michael pursed his lips thoughtfully and said at last: 'It's very late, Red. Why don't you go to bed and sleep on it, mmm? Tomorrow . . .'

'Tomorrow won't change anything and I wouldn't sleep. Why didn't you tell me?'

Michael considered the brandy in his glass, the planes on his face sharply accentuated, the hollows shadowed. 'I thought,' he said, 'that if anyone should tell you, it should be Kit himself.'

'Well, of course he should,' she came back impatiently, 'but that's Kit all over, isn't it? He fully intended to tell us both, I'm sure, and then got caught on the hop. That explains Kit, but not you. You kept your suspicions to yourself and made certain you were around to pick up the pieces, except there were none, which was kind of you, but unnecessary. Thanks, all the same.' When he made no answer her chin lifted and a pale surge of red coloured her face. 'You don't believe me, Michael?' she challenged.

Michael drawled, voice bored, 'Does it matter?'

'Of course it matters! There's nothing so galling as pitying looks when they are completely without foundation—which tonight they were. Everyone seems to think——'

'Not everyone, surely.'

'—that Kit has . . .' she struggled for a word and gave a short laugh, '. . . jilted, I suppose, will do—has jilted me. Well, he hasn't.' Her disclosure didn't seem to have much effect and frustration began to take a hold of her.

'Red, why are you telling me all this?'

'What?'

'You don't have to justify yourself to me, so what has upset you?'

Nicola swallowed and said lamely, 'I don't want you to feel sorry for me.' Her colour deepened and she went on crossly, 'And don't deny it.'

'I admit I was concerned but if it will put your mind at rest,' Michael said, 'I'll take your word,' and he crossed his legs and leaned his head back, eyes closed, listening as John Williams dealt with a particularly difficult passage with his usual expertise.

'But the evidence against is pretty conclusive, is that it?' Nicola compressed her lips and then burst out: 'Don't you ever take anyone on trust, Michael? Can't you stop being a lawyer, just for once?'

He opened his eyes and lifted his head and met her indignant gaze. 'I find it difficult to ignore facts.'

'Facts? What facts?'

'For someone so unconcerned, your reaction to the engagement announcement was rather drastic.'

'Yes, but I ...' She stopped. 'I will have that drink, after all,' and she shot up and padded over to the cabinet, knowing Michael was watching her. Here was the crux of the thing, the stumbling block. How could she say: yes, I was in a state of shock, but not over Kit and Hester, but because I'd just realised I love you, have loved you for a long time without knowing it, and it has taken the past few weeks, living close to you, without childhood blindness covering my eyes, to reveal this to me. No ... she could hardly say that!

'You'd do better with black coffee,' Michael murmured and she said:

'I'm sure you're right,' and took a drink of the brandy. 'That's why I felt peculiar. I'd been knocking the old vino back without realising it and our waltz just about finished me off.'

'You were certainly knocking it back afterwards,' he said dryly.

'How I looked had nothing to do with Kit and Hester. I admit when the news finally percolated through my alcoholic haze I was a bit hurt because he hadn't confided in me, but Kit likes his surprises, doesn't he?'

'You can't have him meaning to tell us one minute, and liking surprises the next, Red.'

'Yes, I can, because both are valid.'

'Do you think,' Michael said, 'that you would like any girl Kit chose?'

'In other words, I'm jealous? Ah, come on, Michael—I admit I don't like Hester, but I never have, so nothing's altered.'

'She always speaks very pleasantly about you.'

Nicola smiled maliciously. 'I'm sure she does.'

'Kit has chosen her. It's never wise to fathom why one person is attracted to another.'

'But you can have misgivings, can't you?' protested Nicola. 'Oh, I can understand why Kit's attracted to her—Hester's beautiful, she has class, she's clever and wealthy—I'm sorry if you think I'm sounding bitchy, but I'm trying to be honest. If there are deeper qualities in her I shall be surprised. Her values are totally opposed to mine and I think she'll corrupt Kit, materialistically, I mean.'

Michael said slowly, 'Kit isn't weak.'

'I know that. His easy-going personality covers a strong stubborn streak and he can dig his heels in when he wants to, we both know that, but Hester appeals to the Aunt Margaret part of him and the Uncle Rupert bit will be pushed under.' She gave a helpless lift of her shoulders. 'But as you say, it's Kit's life to do with as he pleases.' She shot him a bright, intense look. 'All I want you to get into that thick skull of yours is that I'm *not* jealous, I'm *not* heartbroken. Good grief, Michael, do you think if I'd wanted to marry Kit years ago I couldn't have done so? That sounds arrogant, but it's the truth.' She took another drink and went on more slowly. 'We played at being in love, Kit and I, when I was in my late teens, but nothing came of it because I ...' She stopped, frowned, and tried again. 'If I'd given Kit the slightest bit of encouragement he would have slipped from the role of friend to that of lover. I ... found I couldn't.' A movement from Michael made her say, 'What is it?'

Michael said: 'Nothing. Go on.'

She drained her drink and set it down with exaggerated precision. 'We were lucky to be able to pick up our old easy relationship.' Her eyes on the glass she now looked up at him. 'Do you think I've been waiting patiently for Kit to propose all these years? Patience has never been one of my virtues, and I do have some pride! If I loved a man and knew there was no hope, I'd clear off and keep out of his way.' She went over and impulsively knelt by his chair. 'What do I have to do, Michael,' she asked, smiling a little, 'to convince you that I'm not emotionally involved with Kit, short of buying advertising space in the national press?' She paused. 'He's the brother I never had.'

'Rubbish.'

'Oh, why am I bothering!' She flung herself up and round and was moving towards the door when Michael, coming to his feet, caught her hand.

'Don't think me unsympathetic, Red . . .'

She wrenched her hand from him. 'I don't want your damned sympathy, Michael, I don't need it. What I do need is your trust!'

'Which I would give you, were it not for one thing.'

She stopped her journey halfway across the room and slowly turned. 'Oh?' She looked at him warily. 'And that is?'

'Kit himself has frequently told me that you and he would marry.'

Nicola stared at him in amazement. 'Kit said that?' She searched his face. 'You're *not* joking, *are* you?'

Michael held her look, a thoughtful expression on his face, and went to refill his glass, pausing as he held the decanter questioningly to Nicola, who shook her head. She sank down on to the sofa and flopped back against the cushions, puzzled, saying with a frown:

'Why should Kit say that?'

'Presumably he thought it to be true, until Hester changed his mind,' Michael offered, returning to stand by the mantel, looking down at her.

'No.' The word came out instantly and firmly. 'There must be another reason.' She shook her head and gave a laugh. 'Michael, Kit's had hundreds of girlfriends. You know that. We all know that.'

'None serious.'

'Damn it, I haven't lived the life of a nun, either.'

'It was assumed Kit was waiting for you to settle down.'

'Oh my God!' The exclamation came out reflectively. She smiled grimly. 'The only reason I'd ever contemplate marrying Kit would be to put Aunt Margaret's nose out of joint—and that's not a good enough reason, is it?'

'Hardly.' The reply was humorously dry.

'Kit hasn't jilted me, or got fed up waiting for me, or anything else the family might come up with,' she told him. 'There's absolutely no need to worry about me, Michael, honestly.'

He inclined his head in acceptance. 'You'll not be able to persuade the family so easily.'

'Blow the family, they can think what they please,' declared Nicola airily, relief spreading.

Michael's mouth lifted ironically. 'There's something to be said for a shortage of relations,' he observed and Nicola got to her feet, shaking her head.

'Oh, no, I won't have that. You're speaking as one who knows he's well off in that direction and who can choose how much of himself he can hand over.' She tilted him a teasing glance. 'You've always manipulated your family with commendable dexterity, Michael.' She picked up her shoes preparing to go. 'As for me, Kit's engagement and my suspected broken heart will soon become eclipsed.'

'Hum ... we'll have to see if we can give them something else to think about,' drawled Michael.

At the door Nicola hesitated and turned her head to look at him. 'Thanks, Michael.' He raised his brows questioningly and she went on: 'For listening ... oh, for everything, I guess,' and before she said something stupid she gave a quick smile and left him.

In bed she went over and over their conversation, wondering if she could have said anything differently. She dismissed Kit's claim—Michael must have got that all wrong, misunderstood Kit somehow. She wondered if she had really convinced him that she was not heartbroken. Perhaps not, totally, but she had given him something to think about.

She turned over on to her stomach, hugging the pillow. All these years she had been waiting for the right man to come along and sweep her off her feet—refusing to make do with second best—and all the time he was there, right under her nose ... except romantically he didn't know she existed. If it wasn't so bloody tragic, she mourned, it would be screamingly funny.

Michael. She spoke his name softly into the quiet of her room and closed her eyes. She could see him clearly ... the blue eyes, the beautiful mouth, the clean line of brow, nose and jaw. How could someone, in one illuminating flash, become the most important person in one's life, she asked herself, flinging over on to her back. How could a face suddenly leap from being ordinary and commonplace to being beautiful and infinitely precious, and a man's opinions and respect neglible one minute and of the utmost importance the next!

Nicola supposed that she had always been trying to make Michael love her, way back, as a child. If attention couldn't be gained one way, then try another. So she had defied and dared, taunted and jeered, anger being a good substitute for love—it was, after all, a positive emotion, direct and personal.

And how subtly had this discovery crept up on her! A gradual build-up of self-awareness, an insight to her change of feelings steadily growing, breaking down past barriers, peeling away the layers from her eyes so that she was seeing Michael as he really was, and not as she had made him. Tonight, the final layer had been stripped away, exploding the myth and revealing the man.

On the edge of sleep she realised that something positive had come out of it all. She had begun to believe that she would never fall in love, that she was lacking in something. It was quite a relief to find, after all, that she was normal. Slow, blind and stupid—but normal!

Victor glanced, as he always did, into the tea-cup, studied the contents for a few seconds and pursed his lips. Swivelling his glance to Nicola, who was reading a letter she had just received, he gave a pointed: 'Ah-ha!' making the sound significant enough for her to look up.

'What are you ah-ha-ing about, Victor?' she asked, and the pursed lips straightened, then became pursed again, accompanied by a raising of the brows.

'Interesting signs in the leaves,' Victor announced, his eyes sliding her way. 'Something happening, eh?'

'Something's always happening,' Nicola replied calmly. 'Be off with you.'

Ignoring her request, Victor sat down opposite and rested his chin on his hand. 'Wish you'd let me look at your hands,' he said provocatively, snipping a dead cyclamen flower between the precise finger nails of his other hand. 'I've had my eyes on those hands of yours for a long time.'

'I know you have,' grinned Nicola, folding her airmail letter away. It was from her mother and Neil and a generous cheque was enclosed for Christmas. 'I know all about my past, thank you very much, and as for the future, I'd sooner not know.'

Victor gave an exasperated sigh. 'Now you know I never predict the future as such and any palmist who does is cheating. Fate and freewill have equal parts to play and you can make up your mind which you go for.' He shrugged. 'I might be able to show a client something in his hand that governs his future that he can watch out for, work with or against, such as it is, but I do *not* foretell the future.' He dropped the dead flower into the waste bin. 'I don't believe in luck ... it's not a gift that some get and some don't. We make our own luck and have to work at it.' He sniffed. 'Shouldn't have thought you were the sort to worry about the future, Nicola.'

'I'm not,' she replied, 'and I'm not a sceptic, Victor. I do think there's something in the reading of the hand, and the stars, for that matter. In fact,

I could become very interested, but not right now. Right now, at this moment in my life, I'm too busy.'

He grinned suddenly, his usually mournful features transformed into those of a sly pixie. 'A bit scared I'll see too much, eh? Ah well, I already know more than you think.'

Nicola looked at him askance. 'Oh? Do you?'

Victor nodded complacently. 'By the shape of your hands.' He held out his own and without thinking Nicola allowed him to take hers. 'You've got what I call an analytical shaped hand ... the long, rectangular palm, the good angle at the back of the thumb, see? Conic tips to the fingers—that means you've got a creative streak. On the surface self-assured and capable, underneath a bit insecure. Good sense of timing, you don't like being late for anything, you're a planner and you like change, and a bit of excitement, eh?' He stopped and eyed her challengingly.

Nicola laughed. 'You could have got all that from just knowing me, Victor dear, and keep quiet about the insecurity bit, there's a pal.'

He wagged a finger. 'If you went to any reputable palmist who didn't know you, mark my words, he'd be saying the same. As for you being interested in the stars—well, the hand is connected, you know.' He turned her palm upwards, smoothing a finger over each section as he spoke. 'This mount at the base of the thumb, for instance, is the Venus mount—you've got a good firm, springy mount—good energy there ... and the mount below your index finger is Jupiter, and below each of the next three fingers we have Saturn, Sun and Mercury. All of them tell us something different, Venus—warmth, passion, love and hatred; Jupiter—ambition, pride, leadership; Saturn—stability, melancholia; Apollo—artistry, prosperity; Mercury—sexuality, mental alertness, business acumen.' Victor hotched his chair forward, warming to his subject. 'Now this centre of the palm is called the Plain of Mars—it tells us about energy and enthusiasm, and the ability to relax . . . all our physical resources, see? Then right down here, near the wrist, is the mount of Neptune—deals with harmony and communication, that does.'

'Someone once told me,' said Nicola, hooked without knowing it, 'that the left hand is the past and the right one is the future.'

'That's all right as far as it goes,' maintained Victor. 'But hands are changing all the time. Some say the left is what you're born with and the right what you become. What happens to that argument when a person's left-handed, eh?'

'I've no idea,' admitted Nicola.

'The way I see it is this. We all know that the right side of the brain controls the left side of the body, and vice versa. If you are right-handed, then we call your right hand the "major" hand—the active hand . . . the hand of reason and shows how you'll cope in a crisis. The left hand, or "minor" hand is just as important. It represents your responses, your instincts. Now reverse the major and the minor and the whole pattern alters, doesn't it?'

'Yes—I suppose it does.'

Victor, whose attention had been going up and down from Nicola's face to her palms like a yoyo, now homed in to her right hand. 'This is interesting,' he murmured, almost to himself. He brought the palm closer to his eyes. 'See those little crosses, like a star? Looks like you could become famous, or could be a loving partnership—marriage, perhaps, eh? Yes, a star on Jupiter is worth having, my girl.'

Nicola came to with a start and snatched back her hand. 'Victor! You promised!' she accused, laughing even though she was cross. Victor showed a pained face.

'Now then, be fair! All I've said is what might be. It's up to you, isn't it? Sitting back and doing nothing'll get you nothing.' He scraped back his chair and stood up. 'You'll be okay, Nicola—a child of the sun, you are.' He saw her amused look and nodded decisively. 'Born under Leo, aren't you!' It was a statement not a question. 'Now the guv'nor's another kettle of fish altogether. Proper Capricorn, he is . . . but he's got an interesting pair of hands, when he let's me have a butchers.'

'Is he a believer, Victor?' Nicola asked with deep interest and Victor grinned.

'To tell you the truth, I've no idea. Doesn't let on. But I'll tell you this. Over the years I've come to believe that the thirty-fifth year is often an important time in a person's life and the guv'nor comes up for thirty-four next January, doesn't he?' He shot his chair under the table as if he'd made an outstanding point, and grinned. 'We'll wait and see, eh?'

Two days later Nicola received another letter, brief and to the point: 'Friday, lunch—1 o'clock, Ziegfelds. Kit.' Nicola made a note in her diary and thought: about time too.

London was murder in the pre-Christmas rush. Nicola flew into the office to sign cheques and drop off Jennie's present. As she was about to leave she said to her friend:

'By the way, are you and Bill doing anything for New Year's Eve? We're having a party at Bredon House and I should love you to come.'

'Great!' exclaimed Jennie, her face brightening. 'I'm all curiosity to meet these Dalmains of yours—we'd be delighted to come.'

'Good. Eight-thirty-ish onwards,' Nicola said, drawing a rough plan on a piece of paper. 'Follow the Ashwell signs but don't go through the town, turn left at the church and we're about half a mile on, just before the farm.' She looked at her watch and gave a groan. 'Must dash. Have a lovely Christmas. Forget all about work and I'll see you on the thirty-first,' and giving her friend a hug Nicola hurried off to keep her lunch date with Kit.

The head-waiter at Ziegfelds greeted her by name and following him through the dining room, Nicola remembered that first time, with Michael, when Kit had re-introduced them to Hester. Much had happened in those months, thought Nicola, with a pang. Michael had happened . . .

Kit was alone. She saw him before he was aware she had arrived and a faint smile already forming on her lips stilled as she examined him. Staring down into his wine glass Kit's face in repose had a hint of bleakness in the lines of his mouth and the set of his jaw, and his brows were slightly creased. He looked up and saw her and his face cleared. He rose to his feet, breaking out into a smile, taking both her hands in his as he said, 'Nickie, love, you look adorable—in fact, you look a million dollars!'

'I'm certainly not worth it,' Nicola replied, laughing, giving him a kiss on the cheek. 'Hello, Kit.' She paused and asked quietly, 'Is anything the matter?'

'Let me take your coat. Glad you could come.

Michael gave you time off without too much hassle, I hope?'

'I don't have to ask permission, Kit.' She allowed him to help her be seated. 'And Hester?'

Kit seated himself opposite. 'What Hester doesn't know she won't worry about,' he said and Nicola frowned.

'There's no reason why Hester shouldn't know, is there, Kit?'

'Of course there isn't. I don't have to tell her everything though, do I? You've had your hair cut.'

'Only an inch, and don't change the subject.' Nicola broke off as the waiter brought the menu and after they had ordered, she went on: 'You didn't answer me before—what's up?' She grinned, and intoned, 'A friend in need is a friend indeed!'

'Honesty is the best policy,' replied Kit, with due solemnity.

'He who hesitates is lost!'

'In for a penny——'

Nicola laughed and shook her head. 'Not really relevant.'

'Of course it is—and nothing's up.' He studied her face as if memorising every curve and line and said at last, 'I'm sorry I didn't tell you about Hes.'

'That's all right, Kit. I understand.'

'Do you? That's sweet of you. I did intend to, certainly before the Ruby do, then during it, and before I knew what was happening we were pushed into making the announcement that night, quite out of the blue.' Their food arrived and they began to eat. Kit poured more wine and added, 'You must have been surprised.'

'Yes and no. It's time you married . . . it was just a question of who.'

'Michael hadn't dropped any hints? I thought he might have guessed.'

'No. No hints from Michael,' said Nicola. She took a sip of wine. 'When's the big day?'

'March. I want you there, Nick. No flitting off to the other side of the globe, please.'

'I've no plans for doing so at the moment.'

During the rest of the meal their conversation became general and on the way out Kit paused at a table, laughed and said:

'Look who's here, Nick!'

Nicola turned and first saw Geraldine Forest and then Michael, who rose to his feet, his expression cool. Greetings were exchanged, a brief mandatory conversation followed and then Kit and Nicola continued on their way.

Buttoning up his coat against the cold, Kit said cheerfully, 'I wonder if Mike will be making an announcement soon?' and Nicola pulled the fur collar of her coat around her, replying carefully, 'I'm not in Michael's confidence, Kit, any more than I was in yours.'

They parted and as Nicola wandered round the shops, trying to do some last minute shopping, she knew that things could never be the same between Kit and her again. Inevitably so, of course, but Hester, being Hester, would make the split wider, Nicola instinctively knew this, and the times they had met had shown that she was right.

On the train home, the ache in her throat grew and grew and the misery in her heart got heavier and heavier as she thought of Michael and Geraldine. Engagements were catchy things and with little more than one year between them Kit and Michael had done everything together.

The vision of Kit and Michael having a double

wedding hit her and made her laugh, despite her low spirits, for no way would Hester agree to that!

Even though the heating was on in the train Nicola was shivering by the time it pulled into Ashwell Station. She turned the heater up in the Beetle and drove home. When she arrived at Bredon House Cassandra was in the drive with the news that Hamlet had escaped and was missing. With a stifled sigh Nicola parked the car and helped join in the hunt.

Hamlet could have been anywhere and the search was pretty ridiculous, but Nicola couldn't resist Cassandra's beseeching look and although her head, by now, was thumping away like mad, she tramped the lanes, calling and whistling, trying to ignore the falling snow and how awful she felt.

When she finally gave in she made her way back to the house and opening the kitchen door she found Hamlet in his basket being petted by a jubilant Cassandra.

'He was sitting on the step when I got back a quarter-of-an hour ago, Nickie—wasn't he clever to find his way home?'

Nicola nodded, pleased but too exhausted to go into raptures, and suddenly noticed a figure leaning just inside the door, watching her. Michael said:

'He knows when he's on to a good thing, does Hamlet—this billet suits him.' He eyed Nicola's pinched, cold face sardonically. 'It was pointless looking for him.' He glanced from Cassandra back to Nicola, eyes heavy-lidded. 'What a pair of softie's you are,' and he tweaked Cassandra's hair.

'What a pity I haven't a pigtail to pull,' Nicola said tartly, moving across the kitchen. 'I suppose you think we should have left him to get run over!'

She was at the door, aware of a stunned silence and then Cassandra said, bewildered, 'Michael's been driving round looking for him, Nickie,' and as Nicola stalked through the door, she added, 'What's Nickie on about, Michael? I haven't got a pigtail! Oh, I just don't understand grown-ups, sometimes.'

'Don't worry, kitten, age doesn't necessarily bring enlightenment,' Michael replied.

Nicola took a couple of aspirins and picked at her evening meal, refusing to catch Michael's eye. Her outburst had been unfair and unwarranted, but if she couldn't love him then she'd better hate him.

The tree was to be put up that evening. Cassandra carefully unwrapped the decorations, one by one, from their tissue paper and said: 'Oh, here's the dear red robin, isn't he lovely?'

'Some of these must be over twenty years old,' murmured Nicola, perched on the top of the step ladder. 'I can remember going to see Cinderella, my first pantomime, with your parents and afterwards your father brought home this coach and horses for me.' She turned the glittering fairy coach in her hand before attaching it to the tree.

Hammering holly into the corners of the room, Noel said, 'I suppose he was a sort of substitute father to you, Nickie.'

She smiled, stopping her work, pensive. 'Yes, I adored him, and Auntie Joan. As you grow older you realise a lot of things you take for granted as a child. It must have been hard for my mother to leave me here. She knew how easy it is for a child to transfer love and affection to whoever is nearest and your mother was very like mine, in looks and personality.'

'Auntie Adele is a honey, isn't she, Noel?' Without waiting for her brother's reply, Cassandra went on, 'Lucky Michael took pity on us. I daren't think what living with Aunt Margaret would have been like!' and she pulled an expressive face as she hung up another decoration. 'Poor old Michael— what a drag, being lumbered with us.' She stood up. 'I'm going to see if the mince-pies are ready— Victor's making them tonight,' and she left the room.

Noel was silent for a moment and then said, 'It's like you say, Nickie, as you get older you come to appreciate things more, and Michael did take on something when he accepted responsibility for us, didn't he?'

'Yes, he did, but I doubt he'd have done anything differently during these years. Why don't you ask him, if it's worrying you?'

'It's not worrying me exactly, but I do know things are going to change.'

'Oh?' Nicola took another decoration, aware that her heart had begun to thump more quickly. She swallowed and found it painful and the thought did strike her that perhaps she was sickening for something and it wasn't just a deep depression brought on by being love-sick.

'I'm pretty certain he's thinking of getting married fairly soon,' Noel was saying. 'I was cleaning my rugby boots and the kitchen door was half-open and they didn't know I was there— Michael and Victor, I mean. Victor was about to go off to give one of his talks and he asked when Michael was going to let him look at his palms again.' Noel dropped twigs and leaves into a waste-box. 'They change, palms do, all the time, did you know? Anyway, Michael said in a jokey voice that he knew exactly what he was doing and didn't need Victor interfering, that Victor had been on long enough, nagging him, and would he kindly have patience until Kit's wedding was over and done with. One at a time, Michael said.' Noel picked up the box and studied his handiwork. 'So he was talking about getting married, wasn't he? I haven't told Cass. She's not too keen on Geraldine and I reckon that's who it must be, don't you, Nickie?'

Nicola nodded.

'There could be someone else, of course. Michael's away often enough, but he's only ever brought Geraldine home. We'll just have to wait and see. What do you think?'

'What?' Nicola followed his gaze upwards to the holly and said quickly, 'Oh, yes, it looks nice.'

'It's a good year for berries,' Noel observed, and went out to get rid of the rubbish.

Nicola sat quietly, not really feeling anything. Her body didn't seem to belong to her anymore. She was still sitting, the Star of Bethlehem in her hands, when the door opened and Michael walked in. He had changed from his city suit and was wearing a pale blue chunky jumper which accentuated the colour of his eyes. He stood watching her, not saying anything, his expression unreadable, and Nicola stood up and reached high to hang the Star in pride of place. The step-ladder wobbled and she adjusted her balance. Michael's voice, cool, condemning, addressed her back.

'Do you think you should be lunching with Kit?'

'Why not? I have to eat,' Nicola replied flippantly, picking up tinsel and throwing it at the branches.

'You know what I mean.'

Nicola turned her head quickly and had to grab the steps as giddiness hit her. Her voice became sharp. 'Yes, I do, and I shall lunch with Kit whenever he asks me.'

Michael picked up an angel from the box and handed it to her.

'Hester won't like it.' He paused. 'These steps aren't safe.'

'Hester can lump it. I'm not going to change my relationship with Kit. I've nothing to hide.'

'You're asking for trouble, Red.'

She rounded on him furiously. 'You're still not sure of me, are you, Michael? Thank you for your confidence!' The steps wobbled again and trying to regain their solidity she overcompensated, sending the wobble into a direct division of the ways. Nicola went one way, the steps the other. She said a muttered: 'Damn,' and Michael began: 'I told you those things were . . .' before diving for her, becoming entangled with flying arms and legs, the force of impact sending him backwards. The tree trembled and became still, the steps landed gently on the sofa, conveniently sliding shut.

They landed hard on the carpet, Michael first, receiving Nicola's elbow in his ribs, winding him, and Nicola following, cushioned slightly by Michael's body, coming to grief as her cheek thudded against his shoulder.

Apart from Michael's grunt as Nicola hit him and Nicola's resigned: 'Ah!' as she toppled, nothing else was uttered during transit. There was a long silence while both were finding breath.

Nicola was lying across Michael, her hair spread over his face, her legs tangled with his. She groaned and murmured into his jumper:

'A black-eye is what I'll be having for Christmas.'

She felt him laugh. His arm lifted its weight from her back as he brought his hand up to brush the hair from his mouth as he replied, his tone equally doom-laden:

'I thought Christmas was supposed to be the season of goodwill. Do me a favour and stick to ground level, Red.' He gave a great sigh.

'The damn steps were perfectly safe until you gave them the evil eye.' She lifted her head and found herself looking into laughing blue eyes. She was aware that his arm had returned and was joining its mate in holding her, pressure light but secure. She went on huskily, 'I think you sabotaged them.'

Michael, eyebrows rising extravagantly, replied reproachfully:

'Is that the way you speak to someone who literally threw himself into the breach, without a thought to personal safety?'

Nicola began to laugh and then stopped, holding her breath, allowing it to escape with a soft: 'Ouch!' as pain followed the laugh.

The door opened and a voice said, 'I came to ask if you were interested in hot mince-pies, but I can see you're otherwise engaged. Pardon me,' and Victor backed out, closing the door behind him.

'Victor's sense of humour slays me,' murmured Nicola and Michael rolled her over gently on to the carpet. Leaning up on one elbow he asked:

'Anything seriously wrong with you, do you think?' and when she shook her head, he added, looking at her cheekbone: 'I'm sorry, but you're going to have a beauty.' He felt in his pocket and brought out a clean handkerchief which Nicola held to her watering eye.

'I shall tell everyone you struck me and that's why I'm leaving,' she answered. She became conscious of Michael's stillness and lack of response and opened her eyes, feeling the colour rising to her face.

'You're leaving?' Michael's expression and tone were mild.

'Yes.' She sat up, wincing as her body protested. 'I thought so. I don't think it a good idea for the children to get used to me being here, do you?'

Michael brought himself slowly to his feet, flexing his legs gingerly.

'I've asked Jennie to find someone to take my place," lied Nicola, hurriedly planning to do so tomorrow, 'a local woman, if she can. I thought it would save you the bother.'

'Thank you. I'm grateful you've stayed as long as you have. Has another job come up?'

'Sort of . . . and my flat becomes vacant after the New Year. I won't tell Noel and Cass, shall I, until after Christmas?'

'That's probably a good idea.' He held out his hands and after a momentary hesitation Nicola placed her own in them. As soon as she was on her feet she withdrew them, wondering despairingly why the impersonal action on his part was like an electric shock to her. He didn't seem at all put out over her leaving.

Michael peered at her closely. 'Are you feeling all right, Red?'

'I'm fine,' she replied, lying her head off. She felt awful, and if she didn't get away in a minute she'd burst into tears.

'You don't look too good to me.' He put his hand across her forehead. 'You're burning—

obviously you're running a temperature. Off to
bed with you, Red. I'll finish in here and then
come and check you're okay. Go on, to bed.' He
gave her a little push to the door.

CHAPTER SEVEN

ACCORDING to the doctor Nicola had tonsillitis. It was, she thought wryly to herself, rather a drastic way of escaping from Michael. Drastic, and not even successful. He visited the sickroom frequently, checking that she had enough lemon drink, or that she had taken her tablets. Once he had gazed round the room, saying: 'Why do I get the impression that you're like some restless spirit, Red, always moving on? Even as a child you never presumed to make your mark on this room, yet it was yours.'

Not any more, she thought mournfully, still in the throes of her illness, her natural resilience and good sense weakened. I don't want to go any more, but it's madness to stay.

Christmas Eve found Nicola a little better, but certainly not well enough to go to the Keynes dinner party. Michael joined her in the sitting room, prior to leaving, where she would stay for an hour for a change of scene. He was wearing a slate grey suit and a pale blue shirt. His tie was blue with red polka dots. Nicola feasted her eyes on him, veiling her feelings. She was able to admit that the whole thing had farcical overtones, this voracious need of hers. She had been going round for years with this blind spot regarding Michael and now she couldn't keep her eyes off him. The more cynical would call it merely sex appeal but it wasn't totally that. You couldn't separate Michael from what he looked like and what he was as a person . . . he was just Michael. On any other man the shape of an ear wouldn't interest her in the least, the funny way he had of rubbing the lobe when he was deep in thought—the deadpan way he cracked a joke—the amused drawl, all would probably irritate in someone else, but because they were part of Michael they were special.

'Are you sure you don't want me to stay with you?' Michael asked and she gave a laugh, enjoying the pleading tone in his voice.

'You can't get out of going that way—Aunt Margaret would smell a rat! She'll . . .' Nicola stopped short and could have bitten off her tongue in chagrin.

Michael drawled: 'You mean she'll have her suspicions confirmed?' He raised a brow as he lazily studied her. Knowing her face was bright scarlet Nicola decided the only thing was to brazen it out. She laughed and pulled a rueful expression.

'Poor Aunt Margaret, she's been convinced I'd get my claws into Kit for years and now he's safe she's beginning to worry about you. I'd hoped you'd not noticed her interest in us.'

'Over the years I've become acutely aware of what Auntie is thinking. It might not be a bad idea to encourage her,' Michael mused, a malicious hint in the curve of his mouth. 'We need something to keep the family occupied, we agreed, didn't we? How about a nice juicy romance between you and I, mmm . . .?' and he leered at her encouragingly.

Nicola shook her head. 'Much too unbelievable,' she said firmly, pouring herself a glass of iced lemon drink.

'Oh, I don't know—might be fun.' This was dropped into what seemed to Nicola to be an over-long silence. She resisted the strong inclination to lift her lashes and instead took a drink.

'However, I think we already have enough to keep them occupied tonight,' Michael observed. 'The spot-light, if you'll forgive the pun, can fall on Noel instead.'

Nicola's head came up in surprise and she breathed, 'Oh, he's told you. I am glad, Michael.'

'He confided in me last night about his ambitions to become an actor and we shall drop that little pearl of information into the family conversation during the evening. Should give a bit of a stir, eh? Give Aunt Margaret's imagination a rest from ridiculous fantasies.'

She laughed with him, but it hurt like hell. So that's what it was, love between her and Michael—ridiculous! Well, and so it was . . .

'How do you feel about Noel?'

Michael shrugged. 'I'm hardly in a position to preach, am I? I've said I'll give him my support. I can't think why he's allowed himself to get into such a state. I've come to the conclusion he must be frightened of me.'

Distressed, Nicola said quickly, 'Ah, come on, Michael, you don't really believe that, do you? Noel has enormous respect for you, and doesn't want to disappoint you, that's all.'

Cassandra called: 'Michael, we're ready.'

Michael remained still, considering Nicola's words, then smiled wickedly. 'I'll give your love to Auntie,' and giving her a lazy wave of the hand he strolled out.

Victor came in a little later carrying a bunch of red roses artistically displayed in a glass vase. 'Here,' he said, 'a present for you. From the guv'nor.' He put them on the low table by her chair.

Nicola bent to smell them. 'They're beautiful. How kind of him.'

'Hum ... I told him you didn't want to go to the party anyway, but he thought you might need cheering up. How're you feeling?'

'Better than I did,' she admitted, her eyes on the red roses. She said suddenly, 'Victor, do you ever have the feeling that you're on an express train and you can't get off?'

Victor studied her for a few moments. 'Can't say as how I have. I'd stay on, if I were you, Nickie. It could be dangerous to jump off,' and as he left the room, Nicola leaned her head back against the chair and thought bleakly: It might be even more dangerous staying on.

Adele rang on Christmas Day. Once Nicola had assured her that she was feeling much better, she told her that she was leaving Bredon House and moving back to the flat. There was a pause and Nicola went on, 'I can't stay here indefinitely, Mother, can I? I don't think it fair to Cass, she's getting too used to me being here, and to save you asking—no, I haven't quarrelled with Michael, that's not the reason!'

Adele said: 'Darling, you are touchy! I'm so glad you're getting on better with Michael these days. I thought if you ever allowed yourself the chance, you'd find you had a lot more in common with him than you thought. Nicola, we're coming to Europe in the spring. If there's a chance to meet up will you come and see us?'

'Yes, of course,' replied Nicola promptly.

'Lovely. Neil has a definite engagement in Rome and they're trying to fix something either in France or Germany, but I'll let you know what transpires. I'd better go now. Take care, Nicola darling, and happy New Year. Give my love to everyone.'

'Happy New Year to you, Mother, and my love to Neil.' Nicola returned the telephone to its stand and stood deep in thought. She had had the overwhelming desire to confide in her mother but had resisted the impulse. Now was neither the time nor the place.

She lifted her eyes absently and they were held by a photograph on the wall. It had been taken one summer in the garden and she could remember the day clearly . . .

In the picture Auntie Joan was sitting on a wooden garden seat with the three-year-old Cassandra on her lap and Noel, aged seven, was leaning against her knees. Uncle John was sitting next to his wife and behind stood Michael, Nicola and Kit, wearing tennis gear. Michael was holding the racquets and Kit had an arm slung round Nicola's shoulder. The camera clicked just as Nicola had turned to laugh at something Kit had said, so she was looking up at him.

She was almost eighteen, Nicola remembered, and the boys had been early twenties. An age ago! She had been teamed with Michael against his father and Kit, and they had won after some stiff opposition. It had been a close, exhilarating match so that when they won she had flung her arms round Michael's neck, whooping with glee. He had laughed and swung her round, feet off the ground, and they had walked back, arm in arm, victorious, to the clapping of Auntie Joan and her mother, who had been watching. She remembered the feeling of pleasure, this camaraderie with Michael, who at twenty-three and studying for the bar seemed suddenly grown up. It lasted the length of that holiday week at Bredon, but when she met him again some time later he had reverted to his usual cool, distant manner. In self-defence she had become flippant and challenging and they were back to square one.

Nicola lifted her hands and straightened the picture before turning away. She stopped in her stride on seeing Michael watching her from the doorway. Confused by the look on his face, she stammered, 'I ... I was just looking at the photograph.' The peculiar silence lengthened. 'It brings back some happy memories, doesn't it?'

'Does it?' Michael said, 'Don't waste your life living in the past, Red, it never works,' and went back into the room. Nicola stared at the empty doorway, a blank look on her face. She had no intention of living in the past, the present was difficult enough.

By New Year's Eve Nicola was recovered. She had spent all day helping Victor and in the early evening drove Cassandra and Noel to their respective parties. They were to stay the night with friends. Nicola couldn't seem to drum up much excitement for either the party, or the New Year, for both seemed to be linked with severing herself from Michael. After a long soak in the bath she turned her mind to what to wear and finally chose a bright yellow pair of dungarees, teamed with a coffee-coloured tee-shirt. Hair up or down? She decided, down, and brushed it, scowling when it wouldn't go the way she wanted it to, in the end turning away from the image of herself dismissively.

Jennie and Bill arrived early on and Nicola introduced them to Michael. Bill was a dear, but shy, and Nicola waited anxiously to see how he would get on with Michael, wanting them to like each other. She had forgotten Michael's ability to draw people out with such a delicate touch and before long he and Bill were deep into a discussion of skin diving, a sport she would have supposed neither knew much about, but as the conversation ensued she was proved wrong. She left them, Jennie showing deep interest in her host.

The whole of the downstairs was taken over by the party, some of the guests invited by Michael, some by Kit, and some were mutual friends. Nicola wandered in and out of the rooms, keeping her eye on the drinks' situation and changing the tape when the music ran out. Hester was there, of course, with Kit. She didn't mix but stayed with a group of friends, of which Nicola noticed the smooth, blonde head of Geraldine as one of their number. Nicola found herself talking to a man with a voice she recognised from the 'phone, the solicitor, Tim Ralston, he of the attractive Scottish accent. He was good fun and the same height as Nicola if she went shoe-less so she kicked them off and after a while the idea cottoned on and quite a few girls followed suit.

When the dining room was opened up and everyone trooped in for food, carrying back plates laden with delicious Victor-goodies, Jennie grabbed Nicola.

'I don't think I could choose between those Dalmain men, but perhaps Michael comes first—he so reminds me of your hero, Fox. Kit's fiancé, Hester, gave me the big freeze, I don't think I care for her much, awfully smiley-smiley while the eyes tot up everything you've got on.'

'Michael? Like Fox? Don't be silly,' responded Nicola, taking a bite of asparagus flan. Her eyes found Michael and rested on him while she thought frantically of Fox. 'Oh, lor', I think you're right, Jennie. How did that happen?'

Jennie grinned and then asked: 'Has the blonde territorial rights where Michael's concerned?' and she sized up Geraldine, who was talking to Michael in an intimate manner.

'She has indeed,' replied Nicola lightly and Jennie pulled a disappointed face.

As the evening wore on everyone became friendlier and relaxed and bursts of laughter were more frequent. The wine flowed freely and ties and jackets loosened and discarded. Kit pulled Nicola into the hall and began to dance, an energetic number that drew an audience and only finished when they were too exhausted to go on and they collapsed on to the carpet in a laughing heap.

Tim found Nicola a seat and she was glad to catch her breath. The admiring light in Tim's eyes was soothing and they talked about books and plays. He was very attentive, and nice, but he wasn't Michael, and after a while Nicola made an excuse to leave him, feeling guilty.

Later she went into the kitchen where Victor was making a start on the clearing up and said, 'The wine is running low, Victor—do you think we ought to have a few bottles as standby?' Victor grunted assent and disappeared down the celler steps.

Nicola eyed Hamlet, sitting disconsolately in his basket, uneasy with all the noise and people. 'Never mind, poppet,' she told him sympathetically, 'back to normal tomorrow,' and dropped a piece of turkey into his eager mouth. She looked up as the kitchen door opened and was surprised to see it was Hester.

She said: 'Why, Hester—can I get you anything?'

'No, thank you,' Hester replied, as if the idea was ridiculous. 'I want to talk to you.'

Outwardly there existed between Hester and Nicola a pretence of friendship. Nicola knew it to be a sham but consented to the playacting for Kit's sake.

'Talk about what?' she now asked cautiously.

Hester's voice was hard and precise. 'You—and Kit. I think you should know, Nicola, that I am a very possessive woman, and I resent anything to do with Kit that doesn't involve me. I warn you I can be a pretty ruthless adversary if I don't have my way. So this clan business with Kit has to stop—so do the secret meetings at Ziegfelds . . .'

Michael or Geraldine? thought Nicola furiously.

'. . . or anywhere else. Do you understand?'

'I believe I do, Hester,' replied Nicola hotly, 'and I deeply resent what you're inferring!'

'My dear, I couldn't care less what you feel— you are totally unimportant to me. I'm merely warning you to keep away from my future husband.' She gave a hard smile. 'I don't share.'

Although she knew it was wasted breath, Nicola pleaded. 'Don't spoil a friendship that's lasted over twenty years, Hester. For that's all it is. Don't you trust Kit?'

Hester gave an impatient laugh and raised her fine brows. 'I wouldn't trust any man, given the right set of circumstances, and Kit's no exception, but if you were not able to bring him up to scratch after twenty years you can hardly pose much of a threat now, can you?'

'Then why bother saying all this?'

'I've told you. I don't share.' Hester turned to go, her strawberry pink dress swirling round her knees, and paused. 'You're enjoying playing hostess tonight, aren't you? I'd make the most of it, if I were you. Michael's spoken for.' With a curl of the lip she left.

Victor clumped up the cellar steps and shut the door behind him. 'Kit's taken something on there, I can tell you. Knew the minute I saw her hands, mean hands she's got.' He gave Nicola a considering look. 'Sorry, but I couldn't help overhearing. A nasty little madam that, and take a tip from me—keep out of her way as much as you can, she's dangerous.' He rested the carton of bottles on the table. 'Oh, yes, you can smile, you're too trusting. She has more hate in her little finger than you have in your whole body. Now then, where does the guv'nor want these?'

Nicola refused to let Hester spoil the party for her and re-joined Tim Ralston who had friends in New York and they exchanged their reminiscences. She caught Michael's eyes on her now and again but didn't care. She was fed up with Dalmain men, they were more trouble than they were worth.

Tim said, 'Can I give you a ring sometime, Nicola? We could go for a meal or the theatre— I'm not treading on anyone's toes am I? Michael's?'

She coloured a little, saying firmly, 'Certainly not. Why do you say that?'

Tim shrugged, smiling. 'Just have the feeling he's keeping an eye on you.'

'Michael got into that habit when we were children and can't get out of it. No, I hesitated for another reason. I'm going to be very busy for the next few weeks.'

'No-one can be that busy,' Tim said persuasively. 'You'll have to eat.'

She smiled. 'I suppose I shall,' she admitted.

'Then I can ring you?' and when she nodded Tim sat back, satisfied.

The New Year was heralded in and toasted, and gradually the party began to thin out. Victor brought in the coffee and people sat around in groups. Michael began to play the piano softly. Nicola and Jennie found a seat on the stairs and Nicola said, a little sadly, 'Another year gone,' and her eyes rested on Michael.

'I think I've found someone to take over here,' Jennie said, following the direction of Nicola's gaze with interest. 'She's a widow, in her fifties, with a car, and she lives in Ashwell. She doesn't want to live in, but would stay over if needed. Her references are good. I've written her name and telephone number down.' She took from her bag a folded piece of paper, 'You can get in touch with her yourself.'

'Thanks, Jennie,' Nicola said absently, taking the paper.

Jennie sat for a moment, her eyes going thoughtfully from Nicola to Michael and then said quietly: 'You don't want to go, do you, Nickie?'

Nicola shrugged and said, a little impatiently, 'I can't stay forever.'

Jennie said casually, 'It's Michael, isn't it?'

Nicola shot her a horrified look and buried her face in her hands. 'For God's sake, Jen! Is it that apparent?'

Her friend said soothingly, 'No, no—really it isn't,' and as Nicola lifted her head, a stricken look on her face, she went on, 'It's just that I've been wanting to meet Michael for so long—I've been curious to see what he was like and so

I've been more aware of your reaction to him. Nickie, I don't think you've looked at him once, not properly, all evening, and a minute ago you allowed yourself that pleasure and I caught you when your defences were down. My dear, I'm sure no-one else suspects.'

'I hope you're right,' said Nicola grimly.

Jennie was silent, frowning. 'Is it hopeless?' she asked.

Nicola gave a mirthless laugh. 'He doesn't approve of me, Jen, he never has. And then there's Geraldine Forest ...' She stopped and shrugged her shoulders.

Jennie's eyes rested consideringly on Michael who was now playing a medley of Cole Porter's songs, drawing his friends round the piano joining in with the words. 'All I can say is this,' Jennie went on, 'if you haven't looked at him all evening Michael has certainly been keeping his eye on you.'

Nicola thrust her fingers through her hair, a faint colour sweeping to her cheeks. 'Yes.' She struggled for the right words. 'There's a physical attraction between us, it's sort've developed recently. I mean, I know there is on my side, but for me it's more than just that, but for Michael, I have the feeling he's attracted physically even though he doesn't approve of me. He also thinks that I'm nurturing a grand passion for Kit and I keep on getting lectures about that.' She gave a bitter laugh.

'What did he say when you told him you were going?'

Nicola lifted a shoulder dismissively. 'He took it very calmly and matter-of-factly. Deep down he's probably relieved.' She scowled and gave a heavy sigh. 'You can never really know what Michael's thinking anyway—he's so bloodly self-controlled, he drives me wild!'

Jennie said presently, 'They're very close, Michael and Kit, aren't they?' Kit had now joined his cousin at the piano and two pairs of hands were vamping popular songs, the mood changing from the romantic to the lively. 'More like brothers,' Jennie went on pensively. 'I mean, if Michael fancied you, and thought you loved Kit, well—he wouldn't poach, would he?'

'I've never loved Kit,' Nicola said crossly. 'Not in that way.'

'Okay, okay . . . but you say Michael thinks you did, thinks you might still do. Now that Kit's engaged to Hester—well, it rather leaves the field wide open, doesn't it?' She paused and said significantly, 'The question is—on what terms do you want Michael?'

'I don't know,' said Nicola quietly.

'Hey, Nick, come and do your party-piece!' yelled Kit from the piano. Before she knew what was happening room had been made for her on the long piano stool between Kit and Michael and she was taken along, willy-nilly, with laughing encouragement all round. 'We would ride on a bicycle . . .' warbled Kit.

'. . . but we haven't got a bike,' sang Nicola.

'The Vanderbilts are waiting at the club,' crooned Michael.

As the song finished amidst cheers, Nicola, squashed between the two cousins, saw that there were two guests not pleased. Hester and Geraldine. Both were smiling with their lips and sending far from friendly messages with their eyes. Yes, Nicola thought, extricating herself from the stool, it was definitely time she went.

The house seemed abnormally quiet when the front door closed on the last guest. Victor had long gone to bed and Nicola gazed round at the destruction of food and drink and the ensuing debris scattered everywhere through the downstairs rooms. She rescued a plate from half-way up the stairs and took it into the kitchen. When she returned Michael was standing by the piano, one finger picking out a tune.

A drift of words were caught in memory . . . the party's over, it's time to call it a day . . .

Michael looked up and walked slowly into the hall. Nicola said brightly, nervously, 'I've seen to Hamlet. Victor said to leave the clearing up until tomorrow. It was a good party, wasn't it?'

Michael nodded his head slowly, his eyes on her face, searching, as though doing a mental drawing for future reference.

Nicola caught her breath and felt the colour come to her face but she held the bright blue eyes with her own and a curious calm settled over her.

'Why are you looking at me like that, Michael?'

He smiled, a slow, lazy smile. 'Because it gives me pleasure,' he told her gently.

His shirt was unbuttoned to mid-chest, the sleeves rolled up. It was the colour of cocoa and made his arms and face seem more tanned than they were. Dark, limp hair dropped across his forehead and Michael had the air of one pleasantly weary.

The colour deepened in her cheeks. Nicola found she was trembling and took a deep breath, fighting for composure. She gave a soft laugh. 'I think that must be a compliment,' and ran fingers through her hair and looked ruefully down at her crumpled dungarees. 'Couldn't you have told me that at the beginning of the evening?' she asked him severely.

Michael took a couple of paces towards her leaving only a few inches between them. Shoeless, Nicola was obliged to look up into his face. 'Believe me, Red, you look much, much more kissable now.' His hand came up and touched her lips with a finger, 'With your lipstick all eaten off and your nose shiny and tired shadows under your eyes. But I could have told you then how this yellow makes your eyes pure topaz.' His hand moved to take a strand of her hair. He twirled it round a finger, releasing it and watching it spring back into a smooth curve round her cheek. 'I don't believe I've wished you a happy New Year, Red.'

Her lashes flickered a little, but her eyes, though slightly guarded, never wavered from his. 'Perhaps you were waiting until the end,' she suggested, her voice a trifle husky, and Michael's lips curved.

'Saving the choicest morsel,' he agreed with a drawl, amusement kindled in the blue eyes. His mouth was only a breath away as they stood staring at each other, Michael considering her just so, and Nicola waiting, her expression grave, her body poised as if flight could be imminent at any moment.

'Happy New Year, Red,' he said softly, and crossed the threshold of that kiss and brought his lips down on hers, firmly, masterfully, his arms encircling her to cajole each hollow and curve into their rightful place.

It was all very well lighting a fuse to a bomb but quite a different thing being left holding it. Nicola tried desperately to catch at reason—a barrage of instructions zooming in from all directions geared to protection and safety, but all were impotent against the onrush of startled delight and reckless abandonment that swept her up and carried her onwards. She had been kissed in anger and kissed in whimsey by Michael and neither had prepared her for what, she now realised, was an inevitable follow-up. With his arms round her, his hand thrust into her hair cupping the back of her head, his long, lean length crushing her to him, reason disintegrated, and she kissed him back. This was the stuff dreams were made of, and not easily won. Reality was for tomorrow.

Nicola told him much more in that kiss than she ever intended. She had thought she could hold back at first but when his lips seduced her with tiny indulgent kisses that for want of breath played round her mouth, touching lightly, provocatively, at the dimpled corners, seeking the shape and swollen fullness eagerly and insistently, exploring the sweep and curve in delight, claiming the trembling softness once more, she was totally lost.

The trouble with dreams was that they had a tendency to con you into thinking they were reality.

As his mouth drew away from hers, Michael, laughter in his voice, murmured, 'I told you it could be fun.' He put her gently from him, holding her for a few seconds, hands on her arms, as she regained her balance.

Was she going to be able to get up the damn stairs without making a fool of herself? Nicola wondered. How the hell could he pack so much punch into one lousy kiss and stand there looking not one whit damaged? Had she imagined that rapid thumping of his heart beat? It could have been just her own, it was going loud enough for two.

Cover up, you fool, she told herself brusquely. 'And it was, wasn't it?' she replied lightly, and lifted a hand and indulgently restored the fallen hair from his forehead to its rightful place. That done she brought her fingers to her lips, kissed them and then placed them gently against his. 'Good night, Michael,' she said and smiled a smile that she hoped shaped itself with confidence and turned to the stairs. He allowed her to gain the third tread before saying:

'Jennie tells me she's found a new secretary.'

Nicola swung round and stared at him blankly and then collected herself. 'Oh . . . yes, I believe she has.'

'Let's hope she's suitable, mmm . . .? You must be glad to be shot of us all.'

She eyed him warily. He seemed perfectly serious. How dare he kiss her like that and then calmly talk of her going!

'We shall be seeing something of you, though, I trust? You'll not turn into a recluse, will you? The children will miss you and want to see you. In any event, we shall all be meeting up at the wedding.' He paused, and added, as though she might have forgotten whose wedding he was referring to, 'Kit and Hester's.'

It was like a dream she had once. In this dream she was on a stage in a play. She didn't know her words or anything about the play and yet everyone else was confident and word perfect. She and Michael seemed to be acting out a scene in such a play, in which there could be any number of players and at least three different endings. She was too unsure of the script at that moment to give a good performance.

'Yes. Of course. The wedding,' she turned and

walked steadily up the stairs without a backward glance. Michael's floating 'Good night, Red,' she merely acknowledged with the lift of a hand.

CHAPTER EIGHT

'RED? It's Michael.'

Nicola's senses leapt to the sound of his voice and she said with forced calmness: 'Hello, Michael. How are you?'

Pleasantries over, Michael went on: 'I was wondering if you would like to come with me to the Barbican Hall on Friday?'

'Can you wait while I check?' Nicola asked. No good announcing that she'd drop anything just for the chance of being with him. She had some pride. 'Yes, Friday's free—I'd love to come, Michael, thank you for asking me. What's the programme?'

'Umm ... let me see—Grieg, Berlioz and Tchaikovsky. I shan't have time to come over and pick you up, I'm afraid, can you make your own way there? I'll bring you home, of course.' Michael waited for her assurance and went on: 'Say, seven-fifteen in the upper-bar. Until Friday, Red. Goodbye.'

Nicola stood with a silly smile on her face. Lovely, lovely Friday! She penned 'Michael' in red on the calendar and walked back to the typewriter lost in thought. She made no attempt to work and rested her arms across the carriage and lodged her chin on them. She hadn't seen or heard from Michael since the wedding three weeks ago ... a prestigious affair. Morning suit and no expense spared in any direction—Chapman Keynes showing the world and its wife how to put on a show.

Nicola wasn't really surprised to see Geraldine

there, spending most of the day close to Margaret Dalmain, who appeared to have taken Geraldine under her wing. Significant? wondered Nicola.

Michael was best man, and seeing him standing next to Kit in the church brought back all the old longing and insecurity. Hester looked radiant as she walked down the aisle on her father's arm. She and Kit went through their responses with clarity and assurance and the general consensus was that they were 'a lovely couple'.

Michael came up to Nicola at the reception and without any greeting, said curtly, 'Where the hell were you when the photographs were being taken? You should have been on the Dalmain family group.'

Nicola raised her brows. 'You're either blind or naïve, Michael if you think that my face on any photograph will please Hester!'

He was silenced, a nerve working overtime in his cheek. 'The photographer is here now and is going to take some informal photographs. I want you on them. Understand?'

The blue eyes bored relentlessly into hers and she said meekly, 'Yes, Michael.'

He stared at her, long and hard, lips pursed, before saying, 'How are you, Red?'

She smiled. 'Fine, Michael, thank you. Is Mrs Palmer satisfactory?'

'She seems to be. Cassandra likes her, and she's a good secretary.'

Nicola looked around her, voice impressed. 'I've seen three members of parliament, two peers of the realm and at least one millionaire here, and there must be many more distinguished guests I fail to recognise in my ignorance.' She smiled mockingly. 'I feel like a poor relation.'

'You don't look like one,' remarked Michael, amusement taking over his earlier annoyance. He appraised her grey flannel suit with its red accessories, eyes resting on the red trilby hat perched stylishly on her swept-up hair.

She chuckled. 'I saw Aunt Margaret visibly flinch when I walked into church, but I'm used to her disapproval.' She paused, going on with an exaggerated drawl, 'You look rather sweet yourself, Michael,' and their eyes held.

Were they both remembering that New Year kiss? Nicola wondered, beginning to feel flustered despite herself. Michael's reply to that droll compliment was cut off by the arrival of Geraldine who smiled at Nicola and then tucked her arm through Michael's.

'Kit wants to know if you have his car keys, Michael—he's beginning to panic.'

'Then I'd better come and reassure him. Excuse me, Red,' and he allowed Geraldine to take him away. Nicola watched them go, the heightened feeling of being alive, with every nerve end singing during that exchange with Michael, beginning to fade. Was she then only half-alive without him? Not a very optimistic prognosis for the future.

She left before the end of the reception without speaking to Michael again, although she made no demur when Cassandra and Noel fetched her to be photographed. Back at her flat she waited for Tim to pick her up. Being only half-alive had no appeal and Tim was pleasant company. If part of the pleasure was in the fact that he knew Michael and could talk of him, well, she had never promised Tim anything more than friendship.

Friday arrived, wet and windy. Nicola emerged

from the underground, head bent down against the driving rain and hurried towards the Barbican Centre, her heels clicking on the tiled pavement. Once through the entrance doors the warmth and lights enveloped her and she turned down the collar of her raincoat and took off the wide-brimmed rainhat, wiping a strand of wet hair from her cheek with the back of a hand. Michael approached out of the crowd and she said, 'Hello, Michael—what a night!' and gave herself over to the pleasure of being with him.

Michael grinned. 'It is rather dramatic, isn't it? Let me take your coat. I've already got you a drink,' and he handed her a glass.

'How organised you are. Thank you,' she replied and when he rejoined her, Michael cast a lazy appraisal over her.

'How are you, Red? We haven't seen anything of you lately. You aren't going to abandon us completely, I hope?'

'Why, no, I've been busy,' she answered, disconcerted by a brief, sharp light that flickered in his eyes as he replied:

'Not too busy to see Tim Ralston.' It was not a question.

She met his look gravely. 'No.' Her nerve endings began to tingle as the silence between them lengthened. She took a breath and said, 'He often gives me news of you, too.'

Michael lifted his hand and gently brushed away the strand of stubborn hair which had dried on her cheek. 'Poor Tim,' he murmured.

A frisson, delicate and exquisite, streaked through her. A voice over the tannoy echoed round the foyer and Michael took her hand and tucked it through his arm, still retaining his hold.

'Time to take our seats,' he said, and then: 'Are you cold? You're trembling.'

She turned her head and met his gaze. 'Yes,' she admitted, 'but I'm not cold.' She smiled a small smile and Michael closed his hand over hers but didn't speak.

The evening was pure magic. Nicola let the music sweep over her and knew that part of the magic was having Michael by her side, his arm lightly touching hers on the rest, sharing the occasional glance as they appreciated the music together. It was almost as if words were unnecessary between them.

The Tchaikovsky was a fitting end. Swept by the passions of the music they walked out of the concert hall into the night and came to with a start, and laughing, ran to the car. Safe in the dry shelter of the Jaguar laughter died and Michael searched her face, taking in every bit of detail before leaning across to kiss her.

Thought and movement were suspended as pretence exploded into fragments. Drawing away slightly, Michael murmured, 'Beautiful, tantalising Red! I've wanted to do that all evening. Did you know that you have the most incredible mouth?' His lips touched them with barely any pressure.

A droplet of rain fell from the brim of her hat on to his hand breaking the spell. She said, 'Michael?'

He touched her lips with a finger, tracing their outline, before saying abruptly, 'Let's go.'

She sat sideways in the seat so that she could watch him, revelling that she could do so openly, an incredible luxury. Michael knew he was under observation and glanced her way now and again. These glances thrilled her, for there was something in the way his eyes rested on her that belied the quietly controlled exterior. She sat, hardly daring to believe that he had really called her beautiful.

The sleek, white Jaguar sneaked across London, the wipers making smooth arches as the rain cascaded down the glass. When Nicola at last opened the door to her flat she moved quickly inside to turn up the gas fire and light the two table lamps. This done, she turned and felt again the vibrant bond that stretched between them as Michael stood watching her.

She said, a little helplessly, 'Where do we go from here, Michael?'

His face relaxed and he gave a smile, the whimsical tenderness in his expression making her tremble. He walked towards her, discarding top coat and jacket, dropping them over the back of a chair as he approached.

'That rather depends upon you, Red.' He took her coat and drew it from her, adding it to his own.

'Oh?' She ran her tongue over her lips, considering this, leaving them glistening. 'Does it? On what?'

Michael lifted his hands to her hair, drawing it aside and the back of her neck tingled as he bent his head and rested his lips against the exposed flesh, moving his mouth gently down to the curve of her shoulder and back again, warm and tantalising, the tip of his tongue snaking circles and waves.

'On what?' she repeated almost inaudibly, a delicious weakness spreading over her.

'Upon whether I have to duck your right hand.'

She heard the smile in his voice and happiness streaked its tentacles, mingling with that other

aching sweetness that was part of loving Michael.
Her mouth quivered, resisting the smile, holding
on to the moment until the laughter refused to be
contained any longer, breaking out, bubbling and
happy. She brought up her right hand and
smoothed it round his neck, spreading her fingers
deeply through the hair at the base, damp and
springy from the rain. 'Perhaps it would be as
well,' she advised, voice deep in her throat, rich
with amusement, vibrant with the knowledge that
she was wanted, 'if you claimed it.'

Michael lifted his head. 'On the premise, better
safe than sorry?' he questioned, his mouth so near
hers she could feel the breath warm on her skin.
He claimed her right hand and brought it to his
mouth, placing a kiss in the palm, his eyes holding
hers. For a long moment he searched her face for
any signs of indecision, and even then, raised his
brows and asked: 'Red?' and Nicola brought her
other hand to his face and stroked the hard angle
of his jaw, feeling the tension disperse at her touch,
following the movement through until her fingers
reached his tie.

She lowered her gaze, intent on the task in hand.
Tie loose, she started on the shirt buttons and
when they were all free, cuffs as well, she
smoothed her hands across the hard cage of his
ribs, up and over his chest, the short curly hairs
springing to her touch, to draw the shirt away and
over his shoulders, until it slipped down his arms
and dropped to the carpet.

His flesh seemed to be on fire. She could feel his
heart beating as she went into his arms and his
hands stroked her hair. Then she was put firmly
away from him and Michael knelt on the carpet
and lifted one stylish Italian clad foot after the

other, pulling off each boot with ease. Balancing herself with a hand on his shoulder, Nicola twitched up the skirt of her dress and unclipped her stockings, a shy smile meeting his upturned face. Michael carefully unrolled them down her legs, only stopping to plant a kiss on each knee as he came to it. Above him, Nicola worked the buttons on her dress and this fell to her feet, the fine silk slip following. She stepped out of the circle of clothing and Michael caught her to him, saying roughly: 'My God, Red, I've wanted to hold you like this for so long!' and she thrust her fingers through his hair and held him to her.

She woke in the night, unused to sharing the bed and lay watching him, not allowing herself to think of anything beyond the amazing fact that he was there. Michael's sleeping pattern was very alike to his waking one—controlled, quiet and spare of unnecessary movement. She moved her head on the pillow carefully and touched her lips against his shoulder, tasting the salt, feeling the warmth of his skin as she curled herself sleepily round his body.

Later she surfaced out of sleep feeling unusually happy and contented, her body languorous and full of well-being. As consciousness edged nearer she found herself responding to a gentle but persistent feeling that was unbearable and yet infinitely sweet as sensation after sensation lifted her towards final awareness and her lashes fluttered and she breathed: 'Oh, please, please ...' and then she was fully awake to the drift of his hands as he began his true courtship of her.

They had first come together with passionate haste, their union urgent, part of a torrent that

swept both in an extremity of need. Now Michael
gave her the gift of his love, and her body sang
exquisitely to his playing, soared to great heights
where pleasure upon pleasure and laughter and
tears were shared, and mind and body were given
with tenderness and reverence.

Sleep overtook them and it was late in the
morning when Nicola woke to find Michael fully
dressed, putting a cup of tea on the bedside table.
He sat on the bed and kissed her hard.

'I'm sorry, Red, I have to go.' He smoothed the
hair from her face. 'We have a lot of talking to do,
but it will have to wait. I'll ring you Monday
evening, mmm . . .?' His eyes laughed down at her.

'I thought I might have dreamed it all,' she
murmured, not fully awake and he gave his slow,
devastating smile.

'I'm glad you didn't.' He kissed her again and
left her. Nicola curled up in bed happily, and only
then realised she hadn't told Michael that she was
off to France the following Tuesday to see her
mother and Neil.

She spent the weekend in a daze. Invited for
Sunday lunch at the Lambert's, her euphoria was
noticed at once by Jennie and when they were on
their own, she asked cautiously:

'Something's happened, hasn't it?'

Nicola smiled dreamily, face glowing as she
stretched luxuriously. 'Oh, Jen, isn't life wonderful?'

'Michael?' Jennie asked, hardly daring to believe
it, and Nicola nodded, the blood rushing to her
cheeks.

'I daren't talk about it, Jen, it's all so new, but
I'm very, very happy!'

*   *   *

When she walked into Dalmains Publishing on Monday morning Kit said: 'Well, well, this is a surprise, how grand to see you!' He came round his desk to meet her, his face showing his pleasure, brown from the Italian sun. He put his hands on her shoulders. 'Do you realise, Nick, that I haven't seen you since the wedding? And that's too long! In fact, no-one seems to have seen anything of you lately.' He kissed her lightly and released her, backing off to collect a chair. 'Where have you been hiding yourself, eh?'

'I've been busy,' asserted Nicola as she sat down on the chair, propping her briefcase against the leg. 'How is everyone?'

She knew how Michael was. He had telephoned her that morning saying he wanted to hear her voice, that he had two minutes to spare between clients. It was three minutes, long enough to remember her trip to Bordeaux, but she didn't remember, and only did so when she was smiling at the telephone back on its hook.

Kit was saying: 'We're all fine. Hester has started to put Tadwell into shape. We entertain regularly and I've found out what a good organiser she is. Now you've surfaced you must come over, come for a meal, or better still, stay the weekend. Ring Hester and arrange a date.' Nicola smiled and nodded vaguely. Kit said: 'I expect you know all the news from Bredon House?'

'Cassandra keeps me in touch,' Nicola admitted and watched him glance at his watch.

He caught her look and explained, 'Sorry, but you've come at rather a difficult moment, Nick. I'm expecting someone any minute but we can talk until he comes.' He paused. 'Seen Mike recently?'

Hesitation was slight. 'At your wedding,' she

offered, not wanting to talk about Michael to Kit yet. 'Tell me about Venice,' she urged, and honeymoon brought to mind, Kit obliged enthusiastically. After a while he again looked at his watch, and with an: 'Excuse me, Nick,' he pressed the intercom, saying a shade irritably 'Has he turned up yet, Monica?' and frowned at her reply. 'Right. Let me know when he does, will you?' He looked at Nicola and pulled an apologetic face.

'You're like a cat on hot bricks, Kit—are you expecting someone wildly important?' Nicola teased. 'Someone I know?'

Kit flapped a hand. '*No-one* knows him! It's the *Code Name Fox* fellow—N. A. Merchant. I've actually persuaded him that we must meet—at least, I thought I had. He's late.' He ran fingers through his hair, exclaiming softly, 'Blast the man.' He recalled his manners and asked, 'Is this purely a social visit, Nick, or can I help you in any way?'

'I think we can help each other,' she replied, taking pity on him. She lifted the briefcase and opened it, withdrawing the manuscript. She lay it before him on the desk. 'You've been waiting for this.'

'I have?' Kit stared blankly at it, his eyes passing over the title, taking in *Fox on the Rocks* by N. A. Merchant, but his brain refusing to register the significance.

He looked up, voice bewildered. 'How on earth have you got hold of this, Nick? Do you know him?' and when Nicola made no reply, her expression changing from gravity to one in which there was a degree of mischief, he looked down at the manuscript again and then back to her, knowledge dawning, slowly, incredulously. '*You?*

You are N. A. Merchant? I don't believe it!' He sat in silence for a moment. 'Yes, I do.' He gave a yelp of laughter and flung himself back in the chair, a hand to his forehead. Sobering, he sat up. 'My God! Why didn't you tell me before, you wretched girl?'

Nicola smiled. His reaction was more than satisfying. 'In case you wanted to turn it down,' she told him simply.

'But . . .' Kit struggled for words. 'Does anyone else know?'

'Mother, Neil, my partner Jennie and her husband.'

'Mike?'

She shook her head, a stab of remorse shooting through her, thinking: I should have told him before Kit.

'Wait until Father hears of this, and Hester!' crowed Kit. 'Nickie, my pet, you're a marvel!' He shot up from his chair and came round the desk pulling her to her feet, taking both her hands in his. 'Do you realise that the reason I demanded to see this fellow Merchant is because I want to discuss publication in America? You, my girl, have taken off with a bang, and if this,' and he prodded the new manuscript with a finger, 'is as good as your first, then we're laughing.'

'Good.' Nicola grinned, infected by his enthusiasm. 'Kit, just one thing—can we keep who I am a secret for just a bit longer? Please? Promise?'

Kit shrugged. 'Very well—it's been a secret all this time, it can be one for a little longer. Now—can I take N. A. Merchant to lunch?'

'Why not?' replied Nicola, 'so long as I can come too.'

*   *   *

She was packing her suitcase that evening when the door bell rang. Perhaps it was Michael, calling instead of ringing! She ran into the hall and threw open the door. Kit stalked in ahead of her, saying decisively, 'I've read it, Nick, and it's good.' He grinned at her. 'You've done it again, you marvellous girl!' He sat down and dropped the manuscript on the table. 'I sat and read it when I got back to the office and couldn't put it down! This Fox fellow will have all the women falling for him and all the men, identifying! In fact, I'm just that little bit jealous of Fox.'

'Surely not, Kit!' laughed Nicola, and then: 'What are you settling yourself down for? I'm in the middle of packing,' she told him plaintively.

'There's one or two things I want to discuss with you—now I'm here can't you spare half-an-hour?'

Nicola flapped a hand. 'Oh, very well—I suppose you could do with a drink?' She went to the sideboard and fixed them both a drink and for the next hour they talked through various points and when it seemed he was through, Kit said slowly:

'There's one more item.' He turned to the dedication page and tapped it with a finger. 'This might be a little awkward for Michael.' His brown eyes rested on her thoughtfully.

The colour rose in her cheeks but her voice was calm. 'Why?'

Kit rubbed his forehead. 'It's rather a delicate situation, you must see that, Nick?' When Nicola made no reply he tried to clarify his words. 'Surely you've guessed about Mike and Geraldine?'

Nicola took a sip from her glass.

'They came to us for a meal last night and it's

pretty evident that something will come of it, they've been seeing each other for months now. So Geraldine might be a bit touchy about you singling Michael out for the dedication.'

It could be fun, Michael had said . . . and it had been, and might continue to be until he got her out of his system.

'You mean that Geraldine might think that our relationship, Michael's and mine, could be something more than the rather nebulous courtesy title of cousin?'

Kit chuckled, eyes twinkling. 'Well—*I* know that's ridiculous, but Geraldine might not.'

Nicola stood up and moved round the room restlessly, trying for common sense. '*Code Name Fox* was for mother, for obvious reasons. As for Michael, I thought *Fox on the Rocks* might be a nice way of saying "thank you" for allowing me a refuge at Bredon House whenever I wanted one— he . . . Michael said he liked my style of writing, though he didn't know it was me he was talking about.'

'Hum . . . well, I don't know, Nickie . . .'

'Can we leave it for now, Kit? I was going to ask Michael's permission, in any event,' she said, thinking—tonight, I was going to tell him tonight, ask him tonight! 'but I'll think about it before I do, how's that? Will you have another drink before you go?'

Kit looked at his watch and reluctantly shook his head. 'No. No time.' He pushed the manuscript into his case and came over. He took her hands and said: 'I'm delighted about your writing, Nickie. I always thought you'd do something a bit out of the ordinary. I'm proud of you.' He kissed her lightly on the lips, drawing away a little to add gravely: 'You'll always be special to me, you know that, don't you?'

Nicola went into his arms and hid her face in his chest. Dear Kit, he had always been there to comfort her ... and she needed comforting. She felt very vulnerable. Had she been naïve to forget Geraldine?

She gave a choky laugh and began to draw away. Kit said humorously: 'You always were an emotional thing,' and he took hold of her chin and eyed her indulgently, giving a rueful laugh before resting his lips against hers, lightly, once more. It began light-hearted enough, but became more serious very quickly. Nicola pressed her palms against his chest and when she could speak, colour high, laughingly scolded, 'Hey! Let's not get carried away, shall we? I'm not up for the Nobel Prize for Literature!'

Kit, an odd, serious look on his face, laughed and released her. He touched her cheek with his balled fist. 'Take care. I'll be in touch.'

Nicola closed the front door behind him, leaning back against it, face troubled. What on earth had possessed Kit to kiss her like that? She covered her face with her hands and collected herself together. Why is life so bloody complicated? she wondered, and went through to the bedroom to finish her packing. She closed her mind to all the implications of Kit's words and began to sort through her clothes. When the doorbell rang again she gave a sigh and went to open it, with the words, 'Well, what have you forgotten?' spilling forth in exasperated amusement.

She gave a start of surprise and exclaimed: 'Michael!' She smiled, eyes lighting up. 'How lovely! I was waiting for your call, but this is much nicer.' She stopped talking and registered his features. He looked desperately ill and she said quickly, urgently: 'Michael—is something wrong?'

'I've just seen Kit leave,' he said slowly and she stared for seconds, uncomprehendingly.

'Yes,' she said. 'He arrived out of the blue.'

'Are you going to let me in, or are two Dalmains in one evening too much for you to cope with?' The heavy sarcasm brought her to life and now she understood and realised that he was angry, the anger banked down by tremendous self-control. She stood aside and Michael walked into the flat and she followed, a coldness spreading over her.

She said steadily, a little colour tinging her cheeks: 'What do you mean by that remark, Michael?'

'You really should close the curtains before you indulge in a passionate embrace with a married man,' he ground out, and swung on his heel and violently closed the offending curtains.

The colour in her cheeks deepened. There was just enough in that kiss for Nicola to feel guilty—not for the kiss itself, that was none of her doing, but for misjudging Kit. She said, her voice low: 'Aren't you jumping to conclusions, Michael?'

Michael smiled, his face at its most lean and dangerous. 'I'm a lawyer, Red, remember? Deny the evidence of my own eyes?' He gave a short, bitter laugh. 'What kind of a fool do you take me for? You went into his arms as if you'd had a lot of practice.'

'And why not?' she admitted carefully, holding back the anguish. 'You've been convinced all along that Kit and I are lovers, so it shouldn't have surprised you.'

There was a stunned silence and Michael clenched his hands. He said with some effort: 'You admit it?'

Nicola raised her brows exaggeratedly. 'Admit what? That Kit kissed me? You saw that he did. There's kisses and kisses, of course ...' She shrugged. She was playing with fire but didn't care. It was all spoilt anyway—what did it matter? 'Did you kiss Geraldine good night?'

Michael frowned. She prompted scornfully:

'Last night, when you took her home. I presume you took her home? Perhaps you felt *I* might jump to some conclusions if you told me you were dining with her at Tadwell? Especially if I was merely a bit of fun on the side.'

Michael's face whitened. 'For God's sake, Red! I didn't say anything because it wasn't important!'

'I bet it was to Geraldine.'

'I tried to get out of it,' Michael said grimly, a nerve working in his cheek, 'but I couldn't. I suppose Kit failed to tell you that Geraldine's father, *and* Chapman, were also guests, plus a Queen's Counsel and his wife.'

'What a distinguished line-up,' she mocked. 'All in the name of duty. How nice. You really should marry her, Michael, she'd be a great asset.'

'I've never intended marrying her, damn it!'

'And I'm supposed to believe that, am I? All the trust is to be on my side?' The anger had broken and her voice trembled with it. 'Which brings us back to Kit. You can think what you like about Kit, Michael, it's none of your damned business!'

Inside she was crying—oh, but it is, it is, it's everything to do with you!

'I'm making it my business,' Michael said savagely, swinging her round to face him. 'I'll not let you waste your life, if I can help it. Kit's always taken what he wants and to hell with the consequences, but *you*, I thought *you* had more self respect, Red! It seems I was wrong.'

'It seems we were both wrong!' declared Nicola, her eyes bright with unshed tears of anger and hurt, and a voice in her head was screaming—tell him, you fool, tell him! and her pride was answering—he doesn't trust me, how could he think such a thing if he really loved me?

She asked stonily: 'Is that all, Michael?'

His eyes blazed suddenly into hers and he pulled her roughly to him, fingers digging into her flesh as he ground out: 'No, but it's enough,' and crushed his lips down on hers. When he broke the kiss, he went on harshly, a sardonic smile emphasising the cold contempt in his voice: 'I've always known I should keep well away from you, Red, right from the start you were my *bête noir*. I should have trusted my instincts, but you're pretty heady stuff . . . and I'm only human.' He let her go. 'I covet Kit's good fortune, but refuse to share your favours.'

'No-one's asking you to,' said Nicola through clenched teeth. 'Get out of my life, Michael.'

Michael sketched her a satirical half-bow, side-stepped her and left. The front door banged violently.

CHAPTER NINE

BORDEAUX was a charming city and had Nicola
been in a better frame of mind she would have
appreciated those charms a little more. She had
glanced at the guide book during the flight and it
told her that Bordeaux lay on the banks of the
River Garonne, that it was an important wine
centre and a commercial port and a good base for
travellers intent on exploring the Gironda or any
of the other districts of Aquitaine. Even Nicola, in
her numb state, could see as she travelled from the
airport with her mother and Neil that there was
history in the buildings. That the symmetry of the
avenues and squares, the statues and monuments,
and the graceful architecture of the bridges
spanning the river, all added to the visual beauty
of the city.

Adele had given her daughter a sharp look on
arrival but had made no comment on the pale face
and dark hollows beneath the eyes. Once installed
in the suite of rooms that Neil had taken in the
Royal Medoc Hotel overlooking the Monument
des Girondines, Adele explained, 'Neil has a
rehearsal with the orchestra in an hour. It's
convenient here as the hotel is within easy walking
distance to the theatre. If you feel up to it, later
on, we'll walk round ourselves, it's well worth the
effort. Do you want anything to eat, Nicola?'

Nicola shook her head. 'I'll just shower and
change and then we'll go, Mother.' She smiled
brightly to dispel the slightly anxious look in

164

Adele's eyes. 'I should love a long, cool drink, but nothing to eat, thanks.'

'I'll have one sent up,' Adele replied. 'There's a bathroom attached to your bedroom, darling. Take your time, there's no rush.'

Nicola wrapped her arms round her mother and murmured, 'It's good to see you.' Adele gently patted her daughter's shoulder, thinking: I suppose she'll tell me in her own sweet time.

The Grand-Théâtre De Bordeaux was an impressive white colonaded building, whose staircase and interior, their guide told them, were later imitated for the Opera House in Paris. When they had seen all that was to be seen they sat at the back of the concert hall waiting for Neil to finish his rehearsal. Adele squeezed Nicola's hand and smiled.

'We're not expecting you to come to the concert tonight, Nicola, that would be stretching filial duty too far. In any event, you look as though you could do with a good night's sleep. I have seats for us tomorrow.'

Nicola woke the next morning feeling more up to being bright and cheerful, although she didn't think she was fooling anyone. She silently blessed Adele and Neil for not asking any awkward questions for she couldn't have talked about it. Over breakfast she learned that the concert had been extremely well received by the first night audience and she went on to tell them the amusing story of her visit to Dalmains and Kit's astonishment when she handed over the manuscript. Pouring out coffee, Adele asked casually:

'Does Michael know?' It was a perfectly legitimate question and one Nicola should have anticipated, but she hadn't, and the rush of heat to her face was a give-away.

'No. Only Kit,' she mumbled, busying herself with a croissant and Adele raised her brows at Neil who made a negative movement with his head.

That evening, viewing herself rather dispiritedly in the mirror, Nicola wondered about confiding in her mother regarding Michael, but dismissed the idea with a sigh. She knew exactly what Adele would say. She could hear her now: Pride is a dreadful and stupid thing to indulge in, Nicola. Had you explained the reason for Kit's visit you would not now be in the state you are. How can you expect Michael to be of a trusting nature when he deals with rogues, cheats and liars all his working life?

That's what her mother would say if she told her, Nicola thought glumly, and all of it true, but it was also true that Michael evidently thought her to be a rogue, a liar and a cheat. She swept up her hair into a loose knot and stabbed combs in it with more violence than necessary.

She gave her dress hardly a second glance. It was the colour of a peach, softly draped in silk jersey, long sleeved to hide the bruises at the tops of her arms. She closed her eyes, reliving the scene and could still feel the heat of his anger. Well—she had always wanted to pierce Michael's reserve and had done so—twice ... once in love and once in anger. The outcome shouldn't have surprised her. She had known that he was no cold fish, that beneath the cool exterior, built up over the years, was a great deal of fire and energy. What was a broken heart and a few bruises between friends?

She frowned into the mirror and added a little blusher to her cheeks. Apart from the pallor you wouldn't suspect the broken heart, she thought cynically, and quickly outlined her lips. She heard Adele call out:

'There's someone at the door, Nicola, can you go, I'm not ready?'

Neil had already left and they were to follow in a taxi. Coming from the bedroom into the sitting room, Nicola checked her watch, thinking that the taxi was early. She opened the door.

'Hello, Red.'

Michael! The blood rushed to her face. She swung on her heel and made for her bedroom. Michael followed, taking her wrist, staying her progress. She glanced down at his hand and said coldly, 'Do you mind? I'm already covered with bruises where you've recently manhandled me.' His hand slackened and withdrew reluctantly and as she eyed him disdainfully the dull red that swept his face was extremely satisfying.

'I suppose this is mother's doing?' she asked and Michael said:

'In part. I wanted to see you. I rang last night.'

'Who is it, Nicola?' Adele's voice came through the open doorway of the other bedroom.

'I see,' said Nicola. 'She didn't tell me, of course. She knew I'd go the minute I heard you were coming.'

'Red . . .'

'Michael, my dear! So you made it after all, how nice.' Adele came from her room, arms out-stretched, smiling. 'Isn't this a lovely surprise, Nicola?' and she turned a gentle, enquiring face to her daughter before accepting Michael's embrace, kissing him French fashion on both cheeks.

Gazing at him, now that his eyes were not upon her, Nicola was twisted with an agony of longing that left her feeling sick. He looked just the same—

no horns, no cloven foot! Just Michael in a dark
suit looking Michael-ish.

'You didn't tell me Michael was coming,
Mother,' she said challengingly. Adele's green eyes
widened.

'Because I didn't know for sure whether he
could make it, darling. You've settled into your
room, Michael?'

He nodded. 'It's on the next floor. Has Neil
gone?'

'Over an hour ago.' Adele glanced at the flowers
in Michael's hand and, reminded, he smiled and
presented her with one of the corsages. 'Oh,
Michael, how lovely, thank you—I adore orchids.'
She made for her room, calling over her shoulder,
'Pour Michael a drink, Nicola, I'm sure he could
do with one,' and disappeared in a swirl of pale
green wild silk.

Nicola stalked to the drinks' table and held up a
bottle, and on receiving a 'Thank you,' from
Michael, splashed some into a glass, dropped in a
couple of cubes of ice and held out the glass.
Michael came to take it, offering the second
corsage to her.

She hesitated and said flatly, 'I didn't ask you
here, but I'll go through the motions for Mother's
sake,' and took the flowers. Michael studied her
for a moment and said quietly:

'Even a criminal is allowed a defence, Red.'

Her smile showed little pleasure. 'However, I
don't have to listen,' and she walked into her
room. She stood for a moment, trembling, and
taking a deep breath, pinned the camellias to her
dress, the milky whiteness showing to affect
against the peach.

*   *   *

Neil, baton raised, surveyed the Orchestre de Bordeaux-Aquitaine with raised brows and with a downward sweep of the hands the music of Richard Wagner filled the concert hall. Nicola remembered the concert at the Barbican, less than a week ago, remembered the magic of that evening and the happiness that followed, and stared stonily ahead. During the interval, while Michael went for drinks, Nicola said grimly, 'Mother, what are you playing at?'

Adele turned a calm face. 'You mean Michael being her? My dear, what could I do? He telephoned yesterday evening on our return from the theatre and asked to speak with you. I told him you were in bed and he asked how long you were staying in Bordeaux. I told him, naturally, it was no secret, and left it at that. I thought he'd turn up, but I didn't know for certain. Neil booked a room for him provisionally, and ordered a spare ticket. I didn't say anything because I thought you'd do something silly, like leave.'

'You were quite right. I would have,' said her tight-lipped daughter.

Nicola was determined not to be left alone with Michael after the concert but her resolve was needless. On their return to the Medoc he announced he was taking a walk before turning in. He said goodnight to Adele and Neil and when it came to Nicola, floored her by saying:

'Congratulations on the books, Red.' He glanced at Adele. 'You must be proud of your daughter,' and Adele beamed back, replying: 'I am,' turning to Nicola and adding: 'I didn't think Michael knew?'

'Kit told me,' explained Michael, his eyes resting on Nicola challengingly. 'Thank you for the dedication, Red. It's a compliment I'm honoured to accept.' He swept the group a general smiling good night and left them, three pairs of eyes following his tall figure out of the foyer, to see him pause on the steps, hesitating before striding out into the boulevard.

'A dedication? Why, Nicola, darling, what a lovely idea ...' and taking one look at her daughter's face, Adele swallowed the rest of the sentence and making a resigned moue at her husband they rode the lift in silence.

The next morning conversation at the breakfast table was mostly between Adele and Neil with a little help from Michael. At the end of the meal Adele looked from him to her daughter and said briskly, 'I do hope you two are going to be sensible and clear up this misunderstanding there is between you. Whatever's happened cannot warrant such childish behaviour. I take no pleasure in seeing your poker face, Michael, and you, Nicola, are too stubborn to see the wood for the trees ... and you look positively ill.'

'Mother, please ...' broke in Nicola tersely.

Adele went on, ignoring the interruption. 'I'm sorry, I don't usually interfere, but I've watched you two fighting for too many years. It's time you stopped. And now, Neil, you can wipe the grin from your face and have the cases brought down.'

Michael followed the taxi to the airport in his car. As her mother kissed her goodbye, Adele murmured: 'Nicola, darling, don't let your pride get in the way of your happiness. Michael has loved you for years ... no, no, he's never said, but I know him too well. Be happy!' She took her daughter in her arms and they clung together for a few moments before breaking apart.

Neil said gently: 'Goodbye, honey. Keep in touch.' He glanced to where Michael was saying goodbye to his wife, adding: 'How about giving the poor guy a chance to have his say, eh, sweetheart? But don't give in too easy—let him grovel a bit, mmm?' and cautiously handed Nicola his handkerchief and shielded her while she dabbed at her eyes, giving a choking laugh as she did so. Neil smiled encouragingly and took Adele's arm and led her determinedly away.

The hood on the Jaguar was folded back and the April sun was warm and pleasant. When Michael turned the car in the direction away from Bordeaux Nicola shot him a swift glance and then stared ahead. They did not speak, the open top made conversation difficult, and Michael drove swiftly and skilfully towards the coast. Long straight roads crossed flat countryside. At Arès, Michael turned off the main thorough-fare and now the road was lined with woods, mile after mile, until it could go no further and the Atlantic Ocean was spread out before them.

Grand Crohot in April was deserted. The solitary restaurant was closed and the large car-park lining the front empty. In season there would be kiosks on the sands and a swarm of naked bodies lying on the sands but today the dunes and the beach were desolate. The sea was a brilliant blue-green and the breeze, coming from it, whipped up Nicola's hair, teasing and playing with it until she tied it back with a silk scarf.

It was obvious Michael had brought her here to talk and while one half of her wanted to oblige him, the other half wanted to forget all the complications and heartbreak and let the beautiful morning take over. She stood on the top of the dune and looked both ways, the coast stretched out as far as the eye could see. Michael, she knew, was watching her, and she felt her cheeks grow warm. Michael said, 'Shall we walk?' and she nodded and ran down the dune, pulling off her stockings and sandals and walking bare footed through the sand, soft and dry at first and then hard and wet where the tide had been. Michael followed and joined her at the water's edge.

'Red—why won't you look at me?'

Nicola allowed the water to reach her toes and then stepped back. She stared out to the horizon, her cotton dress flapping around her legs and answered with a question of her own.

'How are you able to be here—your work, I mean?'

'Red, will you look at me?'

'No, because if I do I'll be lost, and you know I will be, and there's some talking, some clearing up to be done first.'

Michael pushed his hands into his trouser pockets and stared down at a large stone sunk into the sand. He pressed his foot hard on to it and said: 'I had planned some days leave for this week. I'd hoped to ask you to spend them with me.'

'Before you invited me to the Barbican concert?'

'Yes.'

'You thought I'd drop into your hands like a ripe plum?'

'I hoped to persuade you to marry me.'

She swung round. 'Oh!' She took in the masklike features, the tired eyes, the lines harshly drawn and said furiously, 'You're a fool, Michael, do you know that?'

He gave a faint smile. 'The defence rests on that very fact,' and then she was in his arms, lifting her clenched fists and striking ineffectual blows on his shoulders, half-laughing, half-crying. 'How many times do I have to tell you that Kit means *nothing* to me? *Blockhead!*' and then her arms were round his neck and he was saying her name before his mouth crushed against hers.

Michael, cupping her face, raining kisses on her lips, her eyes, the corners of her mouth, ground out, 'Blockhead? Yes! but you must remember that I'm a poor fool in love and when a man succumbs to that disease he needs to be pitied and humoured because his wits become addled.' He buried his face in the soft curve of her neck. 'Will you forgive me, Red, for doubting you?'

She gave a choking laugh and spread her fingers through his hair. 'You idiot, of course I will. You knew that, anyway. You know exactly how I feel about you—at least, if you don't, you should.' She ran the back of her hand gently down the hollow of one cheek. 'I thought I'd shown you how much.'

'I thought so too, until I saw you in Kit's arms and was blinded by jealous rage.' Michael's searching gaze devoured her hungrily.

Nicola said hesitantly, 'Mother told me, just now, that you've loved me for a long time.' She saw him give a rueful smile and caught her breath. 'Oh, God, what a blind fool I've been!'

'Your mother is a very perceptive lady,' Michael acknowledged, putting an arm round her and they began to walk along the beach. 'Let me put it this way—unrequited love has never appealed to me. When my feeling towards you developed into something that kept me awake at night I made damn sure you wouldn't find out.' He shrugged and laughed at her despairing. 'Why?' and went on, 'I didn't think I stood a chance. The antagonism that had sprung up between us, as children, lingered on much longer for you than for me. And then there was Kit.'

Nicola stopped walking. 'Michael, we always seem to come back to Kit.'

'Because he's always been there, between us, Red,' Michael explained, urging her on. 'No, listen, let me try and explain. For our formative years Kit and I were brought up like brothers. Kit must have thought I was part of his family until he was old enough to understand differently. We did everything together and were taken for twins, although we were total opposites in every way. He was a blond, beautiful child, always laughing—Kit could twist anyone round his little finger and did so, frequently. I was a solemn child, difficult to rear at first, and a smile was a rarity. Like all siblings we loved and hated each other in turn, played and fought, although Kit was never a good adversary, he couldn't be bothered usually, I had to wait for you to come along for that! As we grew up, a pattern emerged—Kit the easy, outgoing, demonstrative child, I the difficult, moody, uncommunicative one.'

He stopped and Nicola prompted, 'Until your father married Auntie Joan?'

Michael nodded and his face softened. 'Joan came into my life and I was part of a family at last. She was wonderful, but you know that—very like your mother. When you arrived on the scene, that first time, I bitterly resented you taking any part of this new security I'd been given and made that historic claim that we were not related.'

'I was all ready to worship you,' murmured Nicola.

Michael groaned a laugh. 'Believe me, Red, I regretted the words the minute they were out, but it was too late. We began to play the parts we'd been allotted—you and I. Now and then we made an attempt to throw them off, but we were touchy devils, weren't we? Wanting to belong and fighting for a foothold.'

Nicola grimaced. 'Don't remind me how awful I was. Something seemed to drive me to act the way I did towards you. I blush for the child I was.'

Michael chuckled. 'You drove me wild, but deep down I admired your pluck and as those early years went by I found myself wanting your friendship, envied what you shared with Kit, but daredn't try for it myself in case I failed. That's all I wanted, at first, your friendship. Then, when I came down from Cambridge and everyone seemed to assume that you and Kit were a pair I was hardly surprised. Do you remember your twenty-first birthday party? It was a couple of months before the plane crash. It hit me then that given different circumstances I'd have gone all out to try and make you change your mind about me. I'd always had a respect for your lively mind and physical courage and now, here you were, stunning and witty and all the young bucks swooning at your feet and I fell head over heels in love with you like the rest of them.'

'I never guessed,' cried Nicola crossly and Michael raised his brows, shocked.

'I should damn well hope you didn't,' he drawled, drawing her back along the dry sand. 'I'd always been good at hiding my feelings and I wasn't going to compete with Kit. Anyone else, but not Kit. I stood on the side-lines and watched you both and thought how well suited you were, and envied your capacity to draw people to you like bees to honey. I thought you'd announce your engagement at that party, but you didn't. Then Father and Joan were killed which put paid to a lot of things. Amidst the complications of my life you drifted in and out, and by this time I'd convinced myself I was over you.' He pulled her out of the breeze behind the concrete observation shelter, left over from the war, and kissed her long and hard. 'I didn't live the life of a monk,' he told her whimsically, 'I wouldn't like to deceive you there, and if someone had come along, a bit like you, who wouldn't have been daunted by Cass and Noel, I *might* have married, but no-one did.' He took her by the hand and began to haul her up the sand-dune.

'Am I allowed to murmer Geraldine Forest here?' asked Nicola with mock severity and Michael stopped.

'We'll talk about her this once and then, no more!' He ran her up the last few yards and rested, both of them catching their breath before setting off along the wooden slatted path across the expanse of dunes. 'Until Hester and Aunt Margaret took a part, Geraldine has only ever been a business colleague. She is good company and intelligent but I have never wished to make her my wife. Is that understood?'

'Yes, m'lud,'

'I was damned annoyed with myself for not seeing what was going on, and then, when I did, I tried to extricate myself gently, but couldn't get out of that last dinner-party. For your information, no, I didn't take Geraldine home; daddy, the judge, did, and I've suddenly realised that all these explanations are making me hungry. Let's go back and have lunch, shall we?'

The first few miles they sat in blissful silence, smiling idiotically at each other every now and then, until Nicola asked:

'Michael, why were you so sure that Kit and I . . . well, that we had an understanding?'

Michael said slowly: 'I asked him, once or twice, why you were both waiting and he said he wasn't rushing you, that you had a lot of living to do before settling down as a publisher's wife and that suited him, as he didn't want to get married himself yet. He said you understood each other perfectly, and would marry at the right time for you both.'

'Why did he pretend?' Nicola frowned, distressed. 'He did sometimes make silly remarks, when one or other of us was recovering from a broken love-affair, sort of joking about us being each other's last resort, but I didn't take any notice. It was just Kit, being Kit.'

Michael lifted the hand nearest to him and brought it to his lips, planting a kiss in the palm before giving it back to her. 'I've thought about that myself, these past few weeks, and I believe he was saying what one part of him wanted to believe. He does love you, in his way, but you don't fit into his scheme of things. Hester does. I think he has been torn in two, fighting his feelings for you . . .'

'Kidding himself that mine were stronger than they were,' suggested Nicola sadly.

'. . . and then Hester turned up, and whoomph! Collision course.'

'You thought I'd be hurt.'

'I thought you'd come back from America because word had filtered through that Kit was seeing Hester.'

'Will they be happy, Michael?'

He shrugged. 'Who really knows? Hester will cope, she's a tough little nut and she'll make sure he'll always come back to her, because of Chapman's money. He'll stray, I'm afraid, it's the way he's made.'

The colour rose in Nicola's cheeks and she thrust fingers through her hair nervously. 'You knew him better than I, Michael,' she admitted, biting her lip and looking at him. 'That kiss you saw . . . it wasn't the kiss of an old friend. It knocked the guts out of me—I was so surprised . . . let down, even, and then you charged in and caught me feeling guilty.'

'We were both too unsure,' Michael comforted. 'Our love was so new, so fragile—I'm afraid the past proved too much.' He turned to smile at her. 'But not any more, mmm . . .?'

At the cross-roads in Mérignac they passed the scene of an accident. Gendarmes were directing traffic round a smashed car and a lorry and the ambulance was admitting stretchers, lights were flashing and whistles blowing. Neither said anything for a while and Nicola put her hand on Michael's thigh, for comfort, saying, 'You never know what's going to happen, do you? There's no time to waste in misunderstandings.'

They went to their respective rooms to wash and met down at the dining room. Nicola suddenly found herself hungry for the first time in three days. When they reached the coffee, she suddenly asked:

'How did you know I was here in Bordeaux? I

hadn't told you I was coming—I kept forgetting.'

'I badgered your friend Jennie,' Michael replied smugly and Nicola laughed.

'I doubt she needed much persuading. Jennie approves of you like mad!' The laughter died and she went on gravely, her eyes devouring him. 'I didn't realise how vulnerable you were, about Kit. I thought you understood how it was between us.'

Michael brought his hand to the table and Nicola unhesitatingly gave hers into his keeping. 'I didn't think I was capable of such searing jealousy as I felt when I saw you in Kit's arms,' he confessed ruefully. 'I'd parked the Jaguar further down the road, I couldn't get near to your place, and began to walk along the pavement when I saw Kit's Mustang outside. It stunned me for a minute and I just stood there. Then you both moved in front of the open window and you know the rest.'

Nicola said softly, 'You were very formidable.'

Michael offered his other hand and Nicola took it. 'After you insisted that Kit meant nothing to you, in a romantic way, I began to think that I could begin to court you—woo you away from thinking of me as a big, bad ogre!' He paused and looked at her quizzically. 'You knew what I was doing, didn't you, Red?'

'I . . . thought I knew,' she admitted a little shyly. 'I hoped I was right.'

'While you were living under my roof I didn't feel justified in taking too big an advantage,' Michael said with a smile, and then, 'I love you, Red. Will you marry me?'

The colour deepened in her cheeks and Nicola said: 'Yes, please, darling Michael!' She could feel the life-force flowing through their hands and

gazed drowningly into his eyes. A smile tugged at
Michael's lips as he murmured: 'You do realise
we're the object of a certain amount of attention
from the staff? All the world loves a lover, so they
say, and the French more than most! Shall I order
champagne tonight and set their minds at rest?' He
thought for a moment. 'On second thoughts,
perhaps if I asked for a bottle to be sent up to my
room now, it would be more explicit!'

The maitre d'hotel, without the flicker of an eye-
lash, bowed them out of the dining room with a
polite: 'M'sieur ... M'dame,' and hurried to
oblige.

It was an excellent idea, Nicola decided, taking
a sip of the champagne and then carefully putting
the glass back on to the side of the bath. The
muted sounds of traffic as it made its way along
the Esplanade des Quinconces and the neighbour-
ing promenades drifted in through the open
window, and she murmured, 'Bordeaux is being
sadly neglected.'

'We'll come again and do an intensive tour,'
Michael promised, reaching for the soap.

Nicola sighed happily. 'There's always something delightfully decadent about love in the
afternoon,' she mused.

She felt Michael's laughter as he added, 'And
drinking champagne in the bath!'

The bath was a large one, but to accommodate
them both comfortably it was necessary for Nicola
to lie back, half-supported by Michael who was
now lazily soaping her, and whose head and
shoulders were resting on the end rim.

'Michael,' said Nicola, and he gave an absent:
'Mmm ...?' 'Why did Kit tell you about my
writing? He promised to keep it a secret.' His

soapy hands were having a hypnotic effect on her and when he made no reply she groaned a laugh and rolled over, the water sloshing down the side of the tub. 'No, I won't be sidetracked,' she scolded teasingly. 'Why did he?' She rescued the soap and began to rub it across his chest, making a satisfying lather on the dark brown fuzz. She flicked water on to his face. 'Come on, Michael—give!'

Chin down on his chest, eyes half-closed, Michael said, 'I hit him.'

'You did what?' Nicola heaved herself upright and sat on his stomach. Michael grunted and evaded a tidal wave that threatened to drown him. She stared open-mouthed and scandalised and protested, 'Michael! You didn't!'

He drawled a mimicking, 'Red! I did!'

'But . . . you hit Kit?' she stammered.

'Like this,' explained Michael, balling his fist and touching her gently on the chin. 'Perhaps not so well placed and a little harder.' He eyed her look of consternation and grinned. 'It's not the first time,' he offered dryly, scooping water into his palms and gently splaying it over her shoulders. 'Don't look so worried, Red, darling, it wasn't a brawl—and was acted out in the privacy of his study.'

'At Tadwell? That Monday night?'

Michael nodded. 'Have I told you how beautiful you are, Red?'

'Thank you, and I shall be glad to hear more on the subject later, but right now we're talking about why it was necessary for you and Kit to come to blows.'

'Oh, it wasn't anything like that,' protested Michael, being fair. 'I merely asked him why he'd gone to see you and Kit laughed and said it was none of my damned business, and I showed him that it was.' He grinned. 'I don't know who was the more surprised, Kit or me.'

Nicola groaned. 'It was all my fault! If I'd told you, none of this would've happened. Michael, I don't want to be responsible for bad feelings between you and Kit.'

Michael ran his hands down her arms and said briskly, 'You're getting cold—come on, let's get out.' He stood up, bringing her with him. 'There aren't bad feelings, Red, I promise you.' He smoothed a finger across the concerned lines in her forehead and wrapped her up in a large towel. 'Kit's no fool. He cottoned on pretty quick,' he told her dryly. 'He showed me the manuscript and, needless to say, I was astounded, and angry with myself—loving you even more, if that were possible, and agonising over how I'd left you.'

'I'd only taken the manuscript in to him that day. Kit only knew it was me when I handed it to him,' Nicola explained.

'So he said.' Michael smoothed a hand round his chin experimentally. 'Do you think I need a shave?' he asked, and Nicola put her arms round his neck and nuzzled his jaw with her face, saying teasingly:

'As it's only me who's in the least bit interested in your chin, I say you'll do.' A long and satisfying kiss followed and Michael murmured, 'What an admirable way of finding out!'

'Were there any knowing looks when you told reception I was transferring to your room?' Nicola asked, delving into the wardrobe for something to wear.

'Certainly not!' responded Michael, shocked, as

he secured links to his cuffs. 'The French have better manners than that.'

Bringing out a deep coral jump-suit, Nicola asked worriedly: 'Michael, what did Kit say when you knocked him down?'

'He didn't actually fall to the ground, you know, Red,' Michael pointed out. 'He kind've staggered a bit. I'm no James Bond.'

Nicola had seated herself before the mirror, taking down her hair that she had secured with a rubber-band while bathing. She peered at him through the mirror and pulled a disappointed face. 'Oh dear, and I thought you were!'

Michael grinned. 'I'm more like your man Fox.' He came up behind her and began to fix his tie, his eyes sliding to her knowingly. Nicola burst out laughing.

'I see you've been talking to Jennie! She's determined that I based Fox on you—and maybe I did, subconsciously.' She lifted her face and Michael obligingly kissed her. 'What did Kit say?' she prompted doggedly.

Michael straightened and took up his suit jacket. 'Nothing, right away. He rubbed his jaw and we looked at each other like wary dogs defending their territory and then he grinned and held out his hand and said congratulations, or something of the sort.'

The telephone rang and Michael went to answer it. He listened for a moment and said, 'Yes, will you read it out, please?' and then: 'Thank you.'

'What is it, Michael?' asked Nicola, slightly alarmed by the stillness of his face. 'A telegram?'

'Well, yes . . . from the office. I left the Medoc number, just in case anything came up.' He smiled rather sheepishly. 'It seems I've been given Silk.'

'Silk?' Nicola wrinkled her nose in puzzlement and then gasped, her face clearing in delight. 'Silk! Michael, you've been made Queen's Counsel?' She flung her arms round his neck. 'Darling, congratulations, I'm so thrilled for you. Michael Dalmain, Q.C.! Clever, clever you!' She became thoughtful. 'I wonder if I could bring my man Fox up against the legal profession? I shall have to give the thought some consideration.'

'I refuse to share you with Fox at this particular moment,' said Michael firmly, and Nicola grinned and replied with suspicious meekness:

'Whatever you say, Michael.'

They left Bordeaux the following morning, travelling north, with the intention of taking a leisurely journey back home. Angoulême, its rampants high above the river Charente—Poitiers, Tours, Le Mans ... Nicola discovered a new delight, exploring these historical cities with Michael, a surprising mine of information. They stayed two days in Rouen and then made for the ferry at Calais.

Their discovery of each other was still so new that the conversation invariably turned towards themselves ... when did you first ...? When did you realise ...? What did you think ...?

Leaning against the ships rails, Michael shielding her from most of the sea breeze, Nicola said. 'There's a sad bit inside me that mourns Kit. It'll never be as good again between us, will it?'

Michael's arm tightened round her. 'Nothing stays the same, Red, but if we all work hard enough, we can build the bit that counts—the family unity.'

Nicola smiled up into his face. The wind had whipped colour into his cheeks and his dark hair was untidily blowing, giving him a decidedly boyish look. She said teasingly, 'A proper Capricorn man, aren't you?' then paused thoughtfully. 'How strange it is that I've never realised how much a family man you are in an unobtrusive way.' She frowned and gave a small sigh. 'I do hope things will be all right between you and Kit.'

'Don't worry about Kit,' Michael told her. 'He'll convince himself in the end that he played a part in bringing us together. Whereas the person who really did that was Cassandra with her darned bat!' He laughed softly and pulled her round so that he took her weight as he leaned against the rail. 'I remember that night vividly! I looked up, expecting to see Miss Golding, and there you stood with a "butter wouldn't melt" expression on your face and your eyes all innocent and that damned kimono showing every wonderful curve of your body! I understood all the song writers who reckon that the heart can stand still. Mine did, then. I knew, finally, that I was never going to get over you. Hamlet was by way of a thank-you to Cassandra for getting rid of Miss Golding.' He grinned and gave her a kiss, quick and hard.

'And I,' said Nicola dreamily, 'found my world had gone topsy-turvy, that a lean hunk of a man with the coolest of blue eyes and the most velvet of voices could make me laugh and send shivers up and down my spine merely by touching me— which, unfortunately, he didn't do often enough.'

'You're darned right, I didn't,' growled Michael, 'I'm no masochist! But I'll make up for it from now on.'

England was enjoying a sunny spell and the lambs caught Nicola's eye as they sped homeward.

Seeing a pretty church as they went through a village, she said suddenly:

'Michael, I don't want a big wedding—in fact, could we run away, do you think?'

Michael grinned and shot her a look. 'I'm all for speed and simplicity, Red, but running away is a little drastic, don't you think? If we see the vicar as soon as possible and get the banns read next Sunday we'll only have to wait the three weeks and then can choose any day of the next week we like.'

'I suppose you're right,' Nicola replied philosophically, 'we'll disappoint too many people otherwise—but I'm only having nearest and dearest mind!' She thought a moment. 'I bet Cass would like to be my bridesmaid.'

'Can you get organised in a month?' asked Michael, voice amused.

Nicola gave a decided, 'I could get organised in a week if I had to. I'll send a telegram to Mother and Neil and find out when they can fly over—they'll still be in Europe.' She laughed. 'Oh, won't Mother be pleased!'

As Michael turned the Jaguar into the drive Nicola cried:

'Oh, look, the camellia is out! Doesn't it look beautiful.' Michael switched off the engine and they sat in silence, both looking at the house and garden with quiet satisfaction. 'Of course,' said Nicola, as they let themselves in, 'I'm only marrying you so that I can live here always,' and then she shot Michael a mortified look in case he believed her. His face instantly reassured her and she went into his arms and lifted her face, murmuring: 'You know I'd live in a wooden hut so long as I was with you.'

'I have no intention of making you prove it,'

drawled Michael and the kiss that began lightly enough changed in intensity, leaving them both breathless and shaken. Michael pulled a rueful smile. 'One thing's for sure, we'll have a pearl of wisdom from Victor. Shall we go in and break the news?'

Right on cue the kitchen door opened and Victor appeared, taking in the embrace, the flushed cheeks and bright eyes of Nicola, and Michael's relaxed, proprietorial manner. He grunted, put on a knowing face and said with mild exasperation:

'And about time, too!'

Enter a uniquely exciting new world with

Harlequin American Romance™

Harlequin American Romances are the first romances to explore today's love relationships. These compelling novels reach into the hearts and minds of women across America... probing the most intimate moments of romance, love and desire.

You'll follow romantic heroines and irresistible men as they boldly face confusing choices. Career first, love later? Love without marriage? Long-distance relationships? All the experiences that make love real are captured in the tender, loving pages of **Harlequin American Romances.**

What makes American women so different when it comes to love? Find out with **Harlequin American Romance!**

Send for your introductory FREE book now!

Get this book FREE!

Mail to:

Harlequin Reader Service

In the U.S.
2504 West Southern Ave.
Tempe, AZ 85282

In Canada
P.O. Box 2800, Postal Station A
5170 Yonge St., Willowdale, Ont. M2N 6J3

YES! I want to be one of the first to discover **Harlequin American Romance.** Send me FREE and without obligation *Twice in a Lifetime.* If you do not hear from me after I have examined my FREE book, please send me the 4 new **Harlequin American Romances** each month as soon as they come off the presses. I understand that I will be billed only $2.25 for each book (total $9.00). There are no shipping or handling charges. There is no minimum number of books that I have to purchase. In fact, I may cancel this arrangement at any time. *Twice in a Lifetime* is mine to keep as a FREE gift, even if I do not buy any additional books. 154 BPA BPGE

Name   (please print)

Address   Apt. no.

City   State/Prov.   Zip/Postal Code

Signature (If under 18, parent or guardian must sign.)

This offer is limited to one order per household and not valid to current Harlequin American Romance subscribers. We reserve the right to exercise discretion in granting membership. If price changes are necessary, you will be notified.

AMR-SUB-3R

Harlequin

Harlequin Romance

The Winds of Winter
Sandra Field

Tender, captivating stories that sweep to faraway places and delight with the magic of love.

Harlequin Presents...

VIOLET WINSPEAR
time of the temptress

Exciting romance novels for the woman of today — a rare blend of passion and dramatic realism.

Sensual and romantic stories about choices, dilemmas, resolutions, and above all, the fulfillment of love.

Harlequin Temptation

First Impressions
MARIS SOULE

GEN-A-2

Harlequin is romance...

INDULGE IN THE PLEASURE OF SUPERB ROMANCE READING BY CHOOSING THE MOST POPULAR LOVE STORIES IN THE WORLD

Longer, more absorbing love stories for the connoisseur of romantic fiction.

An innovative series blending contemporary romance with fast-paced adventure.

Contemporary romances—uniquely North American in flavor and appeal.

and you can never have too much romance.